Praise for Linda Dorrell's Fiction

"Dorrell ably weaves personal stories into the larger story of Southern racial strife, depicting interracial friendships as early, faltering attempts at repairing the breech, rather than easy solutions to centuries of oppression. . . . Her characters are emotionally authentic, and this in itself makes Dorrell's first effort a delight."

PUBLISHERS WEEKLY

"Historical fiction with a kick and some devious surprises."

LIBRARY JOURNAL

"*True Believers* . . . is riveting and highly recommended. Woven into the fabric of a compelling story are timeless lessons on the human spirit and the spiritual/emotional resources of the Christian gospel in the face of physical and cultural obstacles to establishing loving relationships and nurturing communities of faith."

MIDWEST BOOK REVIEW

"The American South of the 1950s is skillfully brought to life in *True Believers*. . . . [The tale] evokes the racial passions of the South Carolina town that will never be the same again as an old church comes to new life."

BOOKVIEWS.COM

"Dorrell's tale is to reading what an afternoon drive is to Sundays: relaxing, interesting, enjoyable. The author's characters are well-developed, and many readers will empathize with them on several levels as they deal with dominating family members and the injustice of prejudice."

CHRISTIAN RETAILING

"There are so many great things in this book that it's difficult to narrow it down in a review."

ROMANTIC TIMES

"A story about faith . . . that tells a richly-textured tale of three unlikely comrades who struggle with the internal and external imbalances of a deeply ingrained belief system."

MORNING NEWS, FLORENCE, SOUTH CAROLINA

"*True Believers* is a tale of truth, healing, and beauty. Dorrell's story flows smoothly and slowly and deeply, like life in the 1950s South. Just beneath the surface, however, are currents that are strong and dangerous. Dorrell handles them nicely, and gives us a story of rebuilding and redemption that will linger long after the book is done."

GRAND RAPIDS PRESS, GRAND RAPIDS, MICHIGAN

"Ms. Dorrell does an excellent job of combining social issues in the '50s with historical background, family jealousies, and relationships. All of these are woven into a fast-moving story that will touch the heart and the memories of those who lived during these times."

THREE RIVERS CHRONICLE, SOUTH CAROLINA

LINDA DORRELL

Baker Books

A Division of Baker Book House Co
Grand Rapids, Michigan 49516

Published by Baker Books
a division of Baker Book House Company
P.O. Box 6287, Grand Rapids, MI 49516-6287

Printed in the United States of America

Library of Congress Cataloging-in-Publication Data

Dorrell, Linda.
    Face to face / Linda Dorrell.
        p.   cm.
    ISBN 0-8010-6425-2 (pbk.)
      1. Women alcoholics—Fiction. 2. Recovering alcoholics—Fiction.
    3. Mothers and daughters—Fiction. 4. Murder—Investigation—Fiction.
    5. Sheriffs—Fiction. I. Title.
    PS3604.O67 F33 2002
    813'.6—dc21   2002005441

For current information about all releases from Baker Book House, visit our web site:
http://www.bakerbooks.com

For my father,
R. P. (Pearlon) Dorrell
(1913–1992)
You were always there

PROLOGUE

THE YOUNG WOMAN was vaguely aware that she lay in a small clearing in the woods. It was daytime now. She had lain there for hours, barely breathing, unconscious most of the time, aware only of slight perceptions in her senses. Birds singing—a mockingbird, perhaps. The cool dew on her skin. The sweet smell of honeysuckle.

Her clothes were gone. He had taken them. He had taken everything except the single pearl that lay in the hollow of her throat.

She had tried to memorize the details of his face: the color of his eyes and hair, the shape of the scar on his right cheek.

It was the face of evil.

As he did those horrible things to her, she tried to remember, until she suddenly realized that although she was trying never to forget, she would never have the chance to remember.

Her chest and stomach hurt from all the pain he had inflicted before leaving her here—at least that part of it was over. Her eyes flickered open for a second, and she glimpsed the speckled sunlight that shot through the trees swaying overhead.

When she closed her eyes, she could still see it, a light as white as clouds.

The light grew brighter as her breathing slowed, then stopped, and one end came so she could begin again in that place where evil has no home.

one

HARBOR VIEW, FLORIDA

THE ENVELOPE WAS TIMEWORN, but Wanda Hunter never tired of reading the card inside. Her daughter, Kendall, had sent it to her for her forty-ninth birthday. A glossy photograph of vermilion tulips in full bloom graced the cover, but it was the carefully inscribed sentiment inside that gave Wanda a small measure of comfort.

> Although we haven't always been close,
> the years have changed us both.
> I hope the time has come
> when you can be not only my mother
> but also my friend.
>
> Happy Birthday, Momma
> Love, Kendall

It appeared Kendall had composed the message herself, in beautiful calligraphy that Wanda admired—two talents she hadn't known her daughter possessed. That wasn't surprising. Wanda hadn't seen Kendall in years; she didn't know if she would even recognize her. Although Kendall had written to her from time to time, routing letters to her mother through various relatives and former neighbors, she had never bothered enclosing a photograph. She also had never been back home. But then, Wanda had never had one until now.

Studying the return address, she wondered if she had copied it wrong when she addressed the letter she had finally summoned the courage to send her daughter. The time had come to apologize for all she had done—and not done—but now Wanda feared maybe she had said too much and destroyed the already tenuous relationship she hoped to strengthen.

She had mailed the letter two months earlier but received no reply. Not that it would be unusual to wait so long. Once, Kendall had gone three years without sending her a word. Wanda castigated herself for not responding—she had been too ashamed and was habitually too drunk to risk disappointing her child again.

But she was sober now and had been for nearly two years. She had attended the meetings, straightened herself up, gotten a job, an apartment, a life. Slowly, Wanda had found her way back to the life God intended for her to live, but for her to live it fully she had to do something that scared her more than the withdrawal she had suffered when she finally stopped drinking.

She had to make amends with her daughter, tell her she was sorry for all the pain she had caused, and find out if she could heal the scars she knew her daughter had to bear.

So she had dug out the card and written to Kendall. Having received no reply, her imagination began to run wild. Maybe Kendall had moved. Perhaps the post office had misdelivered the letter. Or maybe her daughter had experienced second thoughts, and the letter had only excavated all the pain Wanda had caused.

The ringing phone startled Wanda from her ruminations. She was winded when she snatched up the receiver from her bedside table.

"You been out running a marathon again?" It was Lottie Knox, a friend she had made at the Church of the Lord's Disciples, a lively congregation that met in a renovated movie theater downtown.

"Don't I wish. You know what Oprah said about middle age being the best years of your life? That only works if you got a personal chef, a personal trainer, and a personal fortune like she does," Wanda quipped.

Lottie laughed. "Ain't that the truth. What're you doing? Are you going to the fellowship supper tonight?"

Wanda sighed. Lottie had become a dear friend, but she was constantly after her to attend every church function listed on the calendar. Wanda had come late to Christ, but it had already become tiring trying to keep up with all of his church's activities. "I don't think so. I have an early day tomorrow."

"Okay. Just calling to see if you needed a ride. Hey, did you ever hear from your daughter—what'd you say her name was, Candy?"

"Kendall. No. In fact, I was just thinking about her when you called. Do you think maybe I just ought to go see her?"

Lottie was silent for a moment. "How long's it been?"

"Too many years to think about. I don't even know what she looks like now."

"Well, she was about grown the last time you saw her, wasn't she?"

"Yeah, but I was in a drunken haze then. I barely remember what I looked like."

Wanda had spent so many hours trying to remember those drunken years, what she had said and done. She was well aware that those years had been marked by sin—there was no other word for it. Alcoholism is a disease—she knew that much, but that didn't make it an excuse to forget the difference between right and wrong, to violate the Lord's commandments. She felt a sudden rush of guilt.

"You know something, I think I will go to that fellowship supper tonight."

Lottie laughed. "You never know. Your daughter might even show up. We're always getting lots of new visitors!"

They agreed on a time for Lottie to pick her up and disconnected. Wanda wished finding Kendall could be as simple as encountering her at church or the grocery store.

She walked into the living room of her modest apartment to get her photo album, assembled from the few images she had managed to salvage from her migrant lifestyle. Wanda had not only lost memories as she drank; she had lost the repositories of those memories. The first-grade crayon drawings. The report cards. When she was homeless, she had even lost Kendall's birth certificate.

Compiling the album had awakened Wanda to the reality that had been her life. It was almost as if she was viewing the photographs of a stranger's child, not one she had borne herself. She had trouble remembering the special days, the birthday parties, the passages that marked Kendall's life, even though the images were testaments that they had truly occurred. In Wanda's mind, her life had been a blur, and she knew it would take much more than a simple collection of fading snapshots to bring it all back into focus.

Kendall's father had been out of the picture for years. Wanda had stayed with him long enough to bear him a child, but alcohol had taken precedence, even over their marriage. When he left her, she had moved far away, down here to Florida, trying to punish him—she wasn't even sure for what—by making sure he couldn't see his daughter. He could be dead, as far as she knew. She wondered sometimes if Kendall had ever tried getting in touch with him.

Wanda ran her fingers over the photographs of Kendall, frozen in time and place. Seeing her innocent face, she imagined what Kendall's life must be like now that she was a grown woman and wondered whether she had found the happiness Wanda was unable to give her.

So now she decided to put her energy into making contact with Kendall, although she feared her venture might turn into a dead end. But she had to try.

She laid the album and its memories on the shelf and went back to the letter.

I'll go there, Wanda thought, surprised at herself. She had some time off coming and would visit her daughter in person. Maybe if Kendall saw her face to face, she couldn't ignore her, or maybe she wouldn't have the heart to turn her away.

"I'm her mother," she said aloud to the ticking clock on the kitchen counter. "I may have messed up the past, but I'm sure going to try to make up for it."

Two

NEAT ROWS OF APARTMENT BUILDINGS and slab-built houses lined Palm Avenue in Rawlings, a two-hour drive from Harbor View. It seemed like a pleasant neighborhood to Wanda, unquestionably better than anywhere she had ever lived, at least while Kendall was with her. Driving slowly, she searched the numbers on doors and mailboxes until she spotted Kendall's address on a 1930s-era cottage that someone had obviously converted to a duplex. Salmon-hued stucco covered the structure, which was surrounded by a well-kept yard dominated by hostas and pampas grass and accented by a well-established grapefruit tree heavy with ripening globes.

A car was parked in the driveway, and Wanda hoped this was a good sign. She had decided to drive over on a Saturday, thinking she would be more likely to find someone home during the day. Clutching Kendall's card, she sat in the car for several moments praying that she had done the right thing in coming here. When she finally got out, she realized her legs were quaking so that she could hardly stand.

It had been so long since the day Kendall left. Wanda had tried often over the years to remember just what had happened, what had been the final turn of events that had sent Kendall away, but she couldn't remember that day at all. She only knew that she had awakened the next afternoon, hung

14

over, trying to recall something, anything, searching the house for Kendall, only to find all her belongings had disappeared overnight, save for a few outgrown stuffed animals and toys. Kendall was gone. No good-bye, no note, no explanation, only the conclusion that Wanda eventually came to herself— her drinking, her neglect, had finally driven her daughter away for good.

So Wanda had come to face the past, and she realized she was terrified. She hadn't slept the night before, excited about the possibility of seeing her daughter again. Now that she was here, she didn't know if she could go through with it. After so many years of rejecting her own daughter, and of Kendall rejecting her, she didn't know if they could bury all the hard feelings and have any kind of mother-daughter relationship.

The sun beat down on the pavement, and Wanda decided the time had come. *Eternity doesn't give second chances.* Her minister's words of counsel swirled in her head. She smoothed her dress, walked purposefully to the door, and rang the bell. After a few moments of shuffling and a door banging somewhere inside, the door cracked open, and a child who looked about six years old peeked out.

"Hello," Wanda said, smiling and leaning over slightly. "Is your mommy home?" The child was precious. Wanda couldn't help but think that maybe she had a grandchild, that Kendall had married and had children already. More family than she dreamed possible.

A woman pulled the door open. "You know you're not supposed to answer the door," she chastised the little girl, who grinned mischievously and ran back into the depths of the house. "Can I help you?"

Wanda looked at the woman, looking for signs of her daughter. "Are you Kendall Hunter?" She backed away and rechecked the number over the door.

"No, ma'am. She used to live here, but she ain't lived here in some time."

Wanda felt her heart go from pounding to sinking. "Oh. Oh, my."

15

"Are you all right, ma'am? You look a little pale. You want I should get you some water?"

"If it wouldn't be too much trouble."

"You sit over yonder on the swing. I'll be out with something in a minute."

Wanda sat on the porch swing and dragged her feet across the gray-painted floor. In a moment, the woman returned with a tall glass of ice water that Wanda sipped carefully.

"I'm sorry to be a bother. Do you know Kendall Hunter?"

"No, ma'am. I still get some mail every now and then—you know, like catalogs and stuff—with her name on it. Other than that, I don't know where she moved to." The woman suddenly eyed Wanda suspiciously. "Are you some kind of bill collector?"

"No, no, nothing like that. Kendall is my daughter."

"Your daughter." The woman nodded. "She didn't let you know where she was moving to?"

Wanda surveyed the manicured yard before meeting the woman's eyes. "We've had a difficult relationship. It's a long story."

"Yeah, I know how that is. My old man took off, and I'd give my eyeteeth to know where he hauled off to so I could get my child support 'stead of having to work three jobs and put my kid in daycare all the time, gettin' raised by strangers."

"Do you know anyone who might be able to help me? A neighbor or something?"

The woman stuck her hands in the back pockets of her blue jeans. "No, the next-door neighbor ain't much help. He moved in here after I did, and I can't recollect the name of the guy that lived there before him. He was a creepy dude. I was glad when he left." She suddenly brightened and rose from the porch rail. "You know, the landlord would be your best bet. Hang on a minute; I'll go get his address and phone number for you."

"I'd be really grateful for that." Wanda sat alone on the porch for several minutes, chiding herself for jumping to conclusions about grandchildren and a son-in-law. Of course,

16

Kendall had a life, but that didn't mean Wanda needed to go around putting her own expectations and fantasies on things.

Presently the woman returned holding out a sheet of lavender notebook paper. "Here you go," she said, as Wanda took the paper in trembling hands. "I hope he can help you find her."

Wanda handed the woman the now-empty glass in return. "Thank you for all your help. . . . Goodness; I didn't even think to get your name."

"Darcy. No problem. Mr. Davenport's cool. Comes anytime I need anything fixed, or sends somebody over pronto. Best landlord I ever had."

"You've been very helpful, Darcy," Wanda said, walking down the steps.

"You know something," Darcy said, and Wanda turned around to find her looking pensive. "I lost my mama a couple of years ago. Cancer." She came down the steps to Wanda. "You and your daughter might've had trouble, but you're a good mama to come looking for her. I'd give a million bucks and all the back child support in the world if I could have just five minutes more with mine." She smiled and touched Wanda's arm. "Good luck finding her."

"Thank you." Wanda went back to her car, clutching the piece of paper she hoped would bring her closer to a reconciliation. Right now, five minutes for a million dollars sounded like a small price to pay.

MANSIONS SURROUNDED by luxurious palms and professionally designed landscapes typified the landlord's neighborhood, making it a marked contrast from Kendall's. Wanda gaped at the sight. Florida's November weather did little to detract from the exquisite flower beds and lush shrubs bordering the manicured lawns. Wanda wished she had taken time to wash her dusty car before she came. Surely someone would think she was trespassing and call the police.

When she found the address she was looking for, she spotted an older couple kneeling in an area that appeared recently tilled; they were planting annuals that had obviously just been purchased at a very good nursery. They stood at the sound of her car, and the man came over to her now-opened window.

"Can I help you?"

"Are you Oscar Davenport?"

"Yes. If you're looking for a place to rent, I'm afraid I'll have to put you on a waiting list. All my properties are occupied right now."

Wanda turned off the engine and got out of the car. "No. If where I just came from is any indication, though, I can see why they're all occupied." She extended her hand to the man who removed his gardening glove to greet her. "My name is Wanda Hunter."

"Hunter." He tapped his chin. "Hunter. Christine!" He turned to call the woman from the flower bed. She came and stood beside him. "Didn't we have a tenant, last name of Hunter?"

"Kendall Hunter. You remember her—when she paid her rent she always brought us something scrumptious she had baked."

"Yes." He nodded in amused recollection. "Are you related to Kendall?"

"Yes, I am. She's my daughter."

"Your daughter! I should have seen the resemblance. You have the same eyes."

Wanda allowed herself a smile. "I'll take that as a compliment. I just came from her duplex. Well, I mean it's not hers, but, you know what I mean."

Oscar Davenport held up his hand. "You're looking for Kendall." His voice suddenly quieted, and his demeanor became serious as did that of his wife. The switch caught Wanda off guard.

"Do you know where I can find her?" Wanda searched their faces, hoping for the answer she wanted.

The couple looked at each other before Christine answered. "I don't quite know how to tell you this, Ms. Hunter . . ." she began.

"Wanda. Please."

18

"Wanda." She removed her gardening gloves and clenched them between her hands. "One day Kendall just disappeared without a word."

"Disappeared? I don't understand. You mean she moved out without telling you?"

"No, that's not quite it." Christine's voice became strained, and she looked to her husband for help.

"Let's go over here and sit." He led the two women to a small arrangement of chairs beneath a weeping willow tree. "It's strange, what happened. I don't quite know what to make of it myself."

Wanda sat on the edge of the chair and twisted her purse handle. "Please go on," she prompted.

"Kendall had always been one of my best tenants," Oscar said. "She always paid her rent on time, kept a steady job, kept the house and yard neat as a pin. A real perfectionist, that young lady." Christine nodded in agreement. "Then one month she was late with the rent. I didn't think that much of it. I thought maybe she had some kind of emergency. I try to work with my tenants when they're having some sort of setback."

"That's very generous of you to do that," said Wanda. "Most landlords'll kick their tenants out without notice if they miss a payment."

Oscar shook his head. "I don't like doing business that way. I find that if you treat people with respect, they'll treat you with respect in return." He rubbed his palms together. "It didn't concern me too much when we didn't see Kendall—she always came to pay her rent in person instead of mailing it in. Christine and I grew fond of her. You could tell she was trying to make something of herself. Too many young people these days live in the moment, but she was trying to build something for the future. Saving her money, living frugally."

"And she was a wonderful baker," Christine added. "Always baking cakes and cookies and pies. We kept telling her that she should start a bakery or a catering business. I think she was starting to consider it." She looked pleadingly at Oscar.

"When she missed the second month's rent payment, we decided we should go over and check on her, see if she was sick or if she needed anything." He sat silently for a moment, scanning the ground before meeting Wanda's anxious eyes. "No one answered when we knocked. Weeds were sprouting in the flower beds, and mail had piled up in and around the box next to the door. Christine was with me, so we decided to use my key and go inside."

Wanda closed her eyes and prayed silently for the strength to hear the rest of their story.

"When we went inside, we noticed a coat of dust covered everything," Christine said, "like she hadn't been there in a while. We looked around, and it looked like maybe she had gone on a trip. The dishes were all clean and put away, but what little food was left in the refrigerator was spoiled. There were empty hangers in the closet, and things like her toothbrush and makeup were missing."

"My wife notices more things than I do," Oscar said, taking her hand in his. "Much sharper in the gray matter in some areas."

"We became really worried after that, and we called her employer."

"Where does she work?" Wanda asked, trying to hide her growing anxiety. "Did her boss tell you where she was?"

"He didn't know either. Said she left one Thursday afternoon and never came back to work again. Left him high and dry. He didn't know what to make of it. His impression had been about the same as ours. She was trustworthy and reliable. Just not the sort of person who would leave like that."

Wanda couldn't hold back any longer. The tears came, and she dug in her purse for a tissue, holding her head down so the Davenports couldn't see her anguish. Christine came over and kneeled next to her chair.

"I'm so sorry we're the ones to tell you all this," she said.

"We all went to the police—Christine and me, and Kendall's boss. They said they couldn't do anything about it—they said young people pick up and move all the time or disappear for no reason. We questioned the neighbors, but no

20

one seemed to know anything. We thought about hiring a private detective, but we didn't know if that would be the right thing to do. We didn't know enough about her background, her family. . . ."

"Kendall never told you anything about me?" Wanda could barely speak through her tear-swollen throat.

Oscar and Christine regarded each other for a moment before Oscar answered. "She said she hadn't seen her mother in several years, that you and she hadn't gotten along. She said she had forgiven you for the way you treated her—she never went into much detail on that—but that she thought it best that she keep her distance from you."

Christine went into the house and returned with three glasses of lemonade. Wanda stared into her glass and took several deep breaths. "So I take it she never came back."

"None of us ever heard anything else from her," Oscar said. "That was back during the summer. I waited another month, but I couldn't let her things sit there indefinitely, so I put them into a storage locker at a warehouse that I own. I was afraid they'd get stolen if I didn't. Unoccupied houses are a great target for thieves."

Wanda glanced at her watch and noticed it was getting late in the day. "Do you know of a motel where I can check in for the night? I'd like to go see Kendall's boss tomorrow, if you'd be kind enough to give me his address."

"Of course." Oscar went in the house and returned with a pad of paper on which he wrote down the motel's address and the phone number and address of Kendall's boss. He also wrote down a third address.

"What's this?" Wanda asked, barely able to see through her tears.

"That's the address of my warehouse. If you'd like to meet me there tomorrow afternoon, say about 3:00, I'd be glad to let you go through Kendall's belongings, if you're up to it."

Wanda raised her head and managed a weak smile. "I'd like that very much."

"I'm sorry we've been the bearers of such devastating news," Christine said as they walked Wanda out to her car. "Is there anything at all we can do for you? Would you like to stay and have dinner with us?"

Wanda shook her head. "I'll be okay. It's been a long day, and I need to rest and think about all this." She extended her hand to Oscar, then to Christine. "Thank you for being honest with me."

"We thought so much of Kendall," Christine said. "If we can do anything to help you find her, please let us know."

"I will, and I'll meet you at the warehouse tomorrow."

As she drove toward the motel, Wanda realized, ironically, that it was happy hour. She clenched the steering wheel and repeated a line of the Serenity Prayer. "Help me accept the things I cannot change," she prayed repeatedly, until the urge to drink faded and the desire to find her daughter strengthened her resolve, and her determination to put things right became her highest priority.

Three

SITTING ON THE LUMPY MOTEL BED, Wanda wondered what she had been thinking in coming here. Oscar Davenport's information did not inspire her hopes for a joyful reunion—not that she had deluded herself into thinking one would take place. She had watched enough daytime talk shows to know that a reunion could go badly just as easily as it could go well. Old feelings would well up in spite of the sudden tearful bouts of "I'm sorry for how I treated you" or "Let's forgive and forget."

Wanda's churning stomach told her that something was terribly wrong here. The Kendall who would suddenly disappear, ignoring her obligations, was totally at odds with the image of the responsible, thoughtful young woman Oscar and Christine had portrayed. Just from their brief conversation, Wanda had gathered enough insight to know that her daughter had certainly not emulated her poor example. Contrary to her upbringing, Kendall had apparently learned the difference between right and wrong, at least where her obligations were concerned. It seemed Kendall was on the right track—so what happened? Where could she be?

Wanda realized she needed to call her AA sponsor, Mel. She had promised to check in, so she picked up the phone and quickly dialed his number. "Yeah," he answered in his gruff New Jersey accent.

"It's Wanda."

"Oh, hey, Wanda. Excuse my curtness, but I got a sick dog over here, and I just got done cleaning up the latest mess."

Wanda laughed. "Pets'll do that for you."

"For you or to you?" She could hear Mel's tone soften. "How you doing, Wanda? How's your trip?"

Wanda filled him in on her visit with Oscar Davenport.

"You know, Wanda, you may have to face the fact that your daughter don't wanta be found."

"I know that. But how can I make amends for what I've done to her if I never get to see her again?" Wanda fought to keep her voice from rising, but Mel caught it anyway.

"I hear your craving talking there. How have you squelched it?"

"Said the prayer, repeated the steps, breathed deep. I was craving a drink so bad it made my head spin, but I got over it."

"I know the feeling," Mel replied. "You're still fairly recent. How long?"

"Two years' sobriety."

"It's a challenge, Wanda. Staying sober is one of the greatest challenges you'll ever face."

She fiddled with the phone cord before answering. "I don't know, Mel. It's starting to feel like I'm facing another one."

Mel was silent for a moment. "Maybe the one was meant to prepare you for the other."

"Maybe." She realized her stomach was growling. "I better go. My stomach's hollering that it's way past time for supper."

"You better shut it up then. Keep the faith, Wanda."

"I will, Mel. Thanks."

"Anytime."

She hung up the phone, picked up her purse, and walked to the door. If she was going to get through this challenge, it was better to do it on cheeseburgers than booze.

ALTHOUGH SHE HAD CALLED the night before, Wanda waited until after church hours to visit Kendall's former employer at a place called The Boxing Ring. Contrary to its

24

appellation, it had nothing to do with guys—or gals—duking it out but was merely a manufacturer of corrugated cardboard boxes located in an old gymnasium. Kendall had worked there as an administrative assistant to the president, George Pettit. She found Mr. Pettit to be a kind man as well, although he had little to add to what Oscar had told her. It seemed Kendall was one of those people who was universally liked. No one had anything bad to say about her, for which Wanda was glad, but it seemed no one knew much about her friends or habits outside their specific relationship with her.

Pettit referred Wanda to the one person he knew who was a friend of Kendall's, a young woman named Mandy, who also worked in the plant. Wanda now faced another door, behind which she felt she would find either the answers to some of her questions or simply more questions.

A slender young woman answered the bell. "May I help you?"

"My name is Wanda Hunter. Your boss—Mr. Pettit? He said you could probably tell me something about my daughter."

"Your daughter?" Mandy looked puzzled before her expression cleared. "Kendall's mother!" She opened the screen door. "Please come in. I've been looking for you for months, but I couldn't find you."

"You have?" Wanda asked, sitting down on the floral sofa Mandy led her to. The room was extremely neat and feminine, decorated in pastel colors and traditional antiques. "I didn't know I was so out of touch."

"I tried getting your phone number from information, but they said it was unlisted."

Wanda cringed inside. She had experienced so much harassment from bill collectors while she was drinking that she continued to keep her number unlisted out of habit. No wonder no one—including Kendall—had called her. "I'm so sorry. I don't know what I'm thinking. Hoping to be found and then making sure I won't be. It makes you wonder why they let some people out in public."

"Please don't be so hard on yourself. Kendall knew where you lived." Mandy reached under the coffee table and pulled

25

out a photo album. "She told me she was planning to visit you."

"She was coming to see me?" Wanda's heart leapt. "Did she say when?"

"Actually I think she was going the weekend she . . ." Mandy's voice trailed off.

"The weekend she disappeared. I've already seen Mr. Davenport. He and Mr. Pettit didn't have any real answers for me. That's why they sent me here. They seemed to think you might know something."

Mandy shook her head. "I'm just as confused as anyone else. Kendall told me she planned to visit you. She left on a Thursday evening. I remember now because it was Memorial Day weekend, and we had that Friday off at the plant." She flipped absently through the album as she spoke, avoiding Wanda's eyes. "I talked to her right before she left, and we planned to go to the flea market the next weekend." Mandy finally brought her eyes up to meet Wanda's. "She liked taking old things and making them look like new again."

Wanda remembered the shabby furniture they had carted from house to house during their numerous moves. "Considering the way she grew up, I'm surprised she would want anything but new."

"She was very careful with her money. Thrifty, I think that's the word."

"You talked with her before she left?" Wanda prompted.

"Yes, but I never heard anything more. When she didn't show up for work Tuesday morning, I went over to her house. She had given me an extra key in case of an emergency, so I let myself in. Nothing looked out of place, so I decided her visit had gone so well that she had decided to stay a few extra days. She had several weeks of vacation time built up. But then Mr. Pettit said she never called to ask for an extension."

"Did you go back to her house again?" Wanda twisted her purse handle.

"Several times. Her mail piled up." Tears began to trickle down Mandy's face. "I went to the police and tried to report

26

her missing. They said they couldn't take the report; they figured she probably took off with some guy."

"Mr. Davenport said they told him the same thing. *Did* she have a boyfriend?"

"If she did, she kept it a secret even from me, and I thought I was her best friend." At this last, the tears came in a torrent. "I'm so sorry, Mrs. Hunter. I don't know what happened to Kendall. I'd give anything if I did. She was the best friend I ever had in my life. I took her picture around and showed it to some people in her neighborhood, but they said her landlord had already asked about her. Nobody knew anything." She grasped Wanda's hand. "Mrs. Hunter, if anything bad has happened to her, I don't know what I'll do. I know I didn't try hard enough to find her. . . ."

Wanda felt tears rise in her own eyes. "Did she ever say anything about me?" she whispered, taking a tissue from the box Mandy offered.

Mandy dried her eyes and blew her nose before speaking again. "She said you two didn't get along very well when she was growing up. I got the feeling she thought it might have been her fault."

Please God, please don't let her think that, Wanda prayed silently. "Kendall was being too hard on herself. It was my fault. I'm an alcoholic—a recovering alcoholic. I've been sober for about two years now."

Mandy nodded. "I know it's hard. I have some friends who got real messed up with drinking and drugs."

"I never did any drugs, but the alcohol alone just about did me in." Wanda searched for what she wanted to say. "Did Kendall say why she was coming to see me?"

"She just said—and I won't forget this—'It's time we put the past to rest.'"

Wanda sat back on the sofa as a wave of fatigue swept over her body. "That's the same reason I'm here now." She began crying again. Mandy came over and sat beside her.

"Would you like to see some pictures of Kendall?" She opened the photo album again.

Wanda nodded, drying her eyes so she could clear her vision. Mandy flipped pages until a photograph of a lithe young woman with long, dark hair and deep, placid eyes came into view. Wanda gasped. "Oh, she is so beautiful!" She took the album into her lap and stared at the photo for several moments, running her fingers over the face. The woman looked so much like Wanda herself had looked before drinking had taken its toll and prematurely aged her face and body. She had a sudden terrifying thought.

"Did Kendall drink? Please, please tell me she didn't drink."

Mandy shook her head. "I never saw her touch a drop of alcohol. Never, in all the time I knew her, not even if someone practically poured it down her throat."

"Thank God," Wanda said.

"She believed in him, too. In fact, we went to the same church. That was how we met. And she helped me get the job at The Boxing Ring."

Wanda found more pictures of Kendall on the next page, some with Mandy, some alone, some with strangers. Mandy had taken one in the yard of the duplex where Kendall lived. A man stood in the background, but a poor camera focus blurred his facial features. "Who's this?" she asked, pointing to the image.

"Some guy that used to live next to Kendall in the duplex." Mandy went into the kitchen and returned with two glasses of cola. "I tried to find out from him if he knew anything about Kendall—you know, what might have happened—but he was really strange about it. You'd think that living right next door to her he might have known or seen something, but all I got out of him was bad vibes and a weird feeling like he was looking through my skin or something." She shivered visibly, folding her arms against her chest.

Wanda squinted at the photo, trying to make out the man's features. "You don't think he could have done something to her?"

"I don't think so. He was strange, but he didn't strike me as somebody who'd hurt anybody. Besides, there's no way of knowing now."

"Why do you say that?"

"He moved out a few months after Kendall disappeared. No forwarding address or anything." She waved her hand. "He's a dead end. I wouldn't even worry about him. What we've got to do is put our heads together and see if we can figure out where Kendall is now."

Wanda permitted herself a smile. "You'll help me?"

"Like I said, I never had another friend like her. I could talk to her about anything, and she was always there for me, day or night. You don't let friends like that go without a fight."

Or daughters, either, Wanda thought. *Not now. Not ever.*

A FLICKERING FLUORESCENT LIGHT over the deputy's desk made Wanda feel a little dizzy, so she tried to focus on the form he had given her to complete. The Rawlings Sheriff's Department was crowded with desks and people and noise, and it vaguely reminded Wanda of the night she made the decision to change her life. The circumstances had been quite different—she was the one who was lost, and now that she had found herself, it pained her that the search for her daughter was boiling down to placing a few words on a printed form that might wind up in the lost and found itself.

She looked down at the page.

Physical description: height, weight, hair and eye color. She didn't know exactly how tall Kendall had grown or how much she weighed, if she struggled the way Wanda did with those five extra pounds she could never shed. It was hard to tell those details just by looking at the photographs Mandy had shown her.

Date and time last seen.

Years and years ago, she thought ruefully.

Clothing description at the time last observed.

What were they wearing during the eighties?

Destination, if known.

29

Wanda threw down the pen in frustration and looked around for the detective who had disappeared into the morass of criminals and sinners. *So much for victim's rights.* She folded her hands in her lap and waited for twenty minutes until Deputy Mynor returned, wiping his face and hands with a napkin.

"So how you coming with that form?" he asked, a little too jovially for Wanda's mood.

"I need you to go out and talk with the people that knew her. I think they would be more help than I would. I just wanted to get the ball rolling here. My daughter's been missing for several months, and I need your help."

He read over the form and peered at Wanda over his half-moon reading glasses. "She's your daughter, and this is all you can give us?"

"I told you, we're estranged. I'm trying to find her so I can make things up to her," she replied, *but I don't have to justify myself to you and I don't know why I'm trying.*

"I can enter the information you've given me in the computer and put out a bulletin, but unless you've got evidence she's the victim of foul play or something, there's not much else I can do."

Wanda stared in disbelief. "I come in here and tell you my daughter disappeared into the clear blue sky, and you tell me there's nothing you can do?"

"People 'disappear' themselves all the time," he said, leaning back and throwing the form on a pile of folders. "She might've found herself a sugar daddy or went crazy and killed herself out in the woods somewhere. Unless you've got something more for us to go on . . ."

"I thought that was your job, to find information to go on." Wanda picked up her purse and slung it over her shoulder, nipping a detective in the arm as he passed. "My daughter was not the kind of person to go running off with strange men on a whim, and I know she wouldn't have killed herself. She was a good Christian girl with lots of friends and people who loved her."

Deputy Mynor raised his eyebrows and smirked. "Then why didn't they go looking for her?"

Wanda spun on her heel and pushed her way through a crowd of young boys who were being booked on vandalism charges. "Look out—" one of them yelled, appending his exclamation with a name she ignored when she accidentally stepped on his foot. She made it to the door and went outside where she sat in her car hyperventilating until she got herself under control enough to drive to the motel.

The suggestion was ludicrous, and this sheriff's department was a joke. She'd go back and report the man to his supervisor, but she didn't think she could face that room again.

It was clear to her now. If she hoped to find Kendall, she was going to have to do it on her own. *Protect and serve*, she thought as she drove away. *What a crock.*

IT WAS LATE THAT NIGHT when Wanda finally arrived home with a U-Haul trailer full of Kendall's belongings behind her car. She parked in the driveway and dragged herself into the house where she kicked off her shoes and collapsed on the bed.

After leaving Mandy's with a promise to stay in touch and share information, she had met Oscar Davenport at the storage locker, where one of his employees helped them load everything. Furniture, cardboard boxes full of craft items, clothing, CDs—all the accumulated belongings of a young woman facing the best years of her life.

After they finished, she had thanked Oscar for his help.

"Kendall was a special young lady," he had told her. "Christine and I hope you find her."

"Me, too," Wanda had said, hoping she wasn't setting out on a futile journey.

A clue had to be floating around that trailer somewhere—she just knew it. The others had missed it, that was all. It was a clue meant for a mother, and she intended to find it.

The Sleep-Tight Motel
Highway 301, Florida

FOR SEVERAL MONTHS, the car sat abandoned in the motel parking lot. The manager had called the police and had them run a check on it, but no one had reported it stolen. The license tags were missing, which was odd but not unusual; plenty of people drove unregistered cars. The check had turned up the owner, Kendall Hunter, but after looking through his log, Henry found he had never had anyone registered at the motel under that name.

Dust and debris covered the car, and two tires had gone flat. It made the place look junky.

"It's too good a car to put in the junkyard," the tow driver said.

"I ain't got papers for it, and the police can't find the owner," Henry told him.

"I reckon we'll sell what we can off it then. I'll have to call a locksmith to get into it."

"Do whatever you gotta do," Henry said. "It's trashing up the place."

He watched as the driver towed the car away; he was glad to see it go. He hoped no one left any more abandoned cars in his lot. If that girl ever came back— well, this would show her.

four

WANDA'S LIVING ROOM looked more like a flea market gone mad than a place where someone actually lived. Boxes and bags of Kendall's possessions had taken over every available space, overflowing to the kitchen and extra bedroom. Wanda and Lottie collapsed on the couch and surveyed the wreckage.

"You never really think about how much stuff fills a house until you move it all," Lottie said, sipping a tall glass of iced tea with lemon.

Wanda moaned. Her back was killing her. After spending the weekend running around trying to find her daughter, then a full day at work in customer service, followed by two hours unpacking a U-Haul trailer, she didn't know if she would be able to walk the next day. "I never had this much stuff in my whole life," she said wearily, wondering how she could keep it all. No wonder Oscar had put everything into a storage locker. She might have to rent one herself, especially for the furniture, which now left her little more than a pathway through her own place.

Lottie leaned forward and peered into a box. "I tell you one thing," she said, "your daughter sure had good taste."

"I wish everybody would quit talking about Kendall in the past tense!" She stomped around the boxes, waving her arms.

"Just because I haven't found her doesn't mean she might not be alive."

Lottie got up and made her way through the maze to her friend. "I'm sorry, hon. I didn't mean . . ."

"No one means to say she's dead. Everyone acts like I haven't had that thought myself!" Wanda tried blinking back her tears and failed. "I know it looks bad. I'm as scared as anybody. It's like there's all this stuff that's unsaid, like no one wants to say that something bad happened to my daughter. But I can see it in everybody's face, including yours." She dug into her pocket for a tissue. "I can even see it in my own face."

Lottie took her by the hand and led her back to the sofa, the only clear seats in the room. "Hon, you'll find her. If she were my daughter, I'd be turning over rocks, too."

Wanda pulled away and took a sip of tea. It had taken a long time to get used to the taste of something cold in a glass that wasn't alcohol-based. For so many years, booze had been breakfast, lunch, dinner, and snacks all rolled into one. She looked at Lottie, who was gazing at her with an expression she had come to treasure, revealing the love of a true friend. "I don't know what I'd do without you, sister."

Lottie smiled. "No, you don't. I'm indispensable. How many other people would help you unload a U-Haul trailer at eleven o'clock on a Monday night?"

They laughed for a moment before leaning back and inspecting the surrounding mess. "So, you want to help me unpack?" Wanda shot her friend a sly grin.

"Indispensability has its limits," Lottie said, rising and taking her glass to the kitchen. "I hate to tell you, but we both have to work tomorrow."

Wanda hugged her and walked her to the door. "Thank you for helping me. I don't know how I'll repay you, but I'll do something good for you sometime."

"You do something good for me every day just by being alive," Lottie said, walking into the darkness.

Wanda bolted the door, then picked up a box from the coffee table. Using scissors, she cut away the packing tape and looked inside, where she found a white teddy bear that was missing an eye and an ear. She held the bear, staring at it, amazed that Kendall still had it.

THEY HAD BEEN LIVING in a trailer house so far out in the country that it didn't even have running water. Wanda's latest boyfriend had left her without any means of support. It was Christmas.

She went on welfare, the first of many times. She decided she couldn't drink and hold down a job, too, as a means of justifying her actions. Welfare would allow her to stay home with Kendall. At least when she wasn't seeking out the nearest bar, the next buzz.

When the check came, her first instinct was to make a trip to the liquor store. Yet the Christmas lights were dangling over the streets, and Kendall was jumping up and down, raving about Santa Claus. She was still young enough to believe then. So Wanda did something she didn't usually do.

She went to the grocery store and filled her cart with food—a turkey and all the fixings, along with ingredients for fudge and cake and pie. In a rare act of self-control, she allowed herself one bottle of wine. Then she went to the discount store and, while Kendall waited in the car, bought gifts—a doll and the teddy bear. And gift wrap.

That weekend they celebrated like a normal family. She remembered the look on Kendall's face when she opened the bear. Although she was seven, Kendall and the bear—she named it Tony—went everywhere together.

WANDA HUGGED THE BEAR to her chest. She guessed it was one of the few normal things Kendall had ever owned when she was growing up, the only possession that made her feel that she was like the other children. Keeping it must have been her way of holding onto the one thing, one holiday that made her mother seem like the other children's mothers.

In her bedroom, Wanda placed the bear in the middle of her bed and knelt. "Lord," she prayed, "I'm so sorry for what I did to my daughter. I messed up bad, and I hope you'll give me the chance to make it up to her. If there's anything in all this mess to tell me where she is, please help me find it. I gotta make it up to her, Lord. I need to make it right."

She laid down fully clothed, exhausted, desperately hoping she would get her second chance, no matter how long or what it might take. She was going to find Kendall. Her life—and Kendall's, too—depended on it.

THE NEXT MORNING, Wanda woke feeling oddly at peace. It didn't make sense. She was only beginning her search, only beginning to get to know the woman that was her daughter, not the child she remembered, if only vaguely. As she prepared breakfast, she kept glancing at the piles of boxes, thinking that here she had her daughter, if only partially.

Possessions tell stories about people, Wanda had discovered. Certainly the lack of them told so much about herself, she often thought. Moving from house to trailer to apartments to shelters to places she could scarcely recall, when there wasn't money or sobriety enough to make a home.

A home. That was something else she had never given Kendall. It preyed on Wanda's heart that what came so simply to others was so difficult for her. Even when she had managed to stay away from the bottle, it took everything she could scrape together just to pay herself out of the debt she accrued during her binges. She had never gotten ahead until now.

When she had finally decided to stop drinking, truly stop, she realized the price they had all paid. Although she was the only one who drank, the contents of all those bottles had drowned everyone around her in pain.

When she finished dressing, she noticed the time. Plenty of time to make it to a meeting.

She drove the three miles to the old Episcopal church that loaned the use of its fellowship hall to their group three mornings a week. Inside, a group of about fifteen women, the Sisters of Serenity AA group, had gathered and were giving the coffee machine a workout. Wanda belonged to this women-only group and another generic group, consisting of men and women from all the social and economic strata of central

Florida. That was where she had met Mel, her sponsor. She herself had not reached the stage where she felt she could sponsor someone else, and it was her personal goal. The organization had helped keep her sober. She had talked it out so often. Alcoholism was a bottomless pit of stories, it seemed. Universal, yet different, like grief and love. She sat on a hard folding chair and asked to speak first.

"I'm trying to find my daughter, Kendall, to make amends for all that I put her through," she began, looking around at the faces she had grown to know, mostly by only first names, some more intimately. "I went to see her this past weekend, only to find that she's disappeared."

Looks of concern rippled across the women's faces. "Explain what you mean, Wanda." Mona was the group's ersatz leader, the one with the longest record of sobriety, twenty-five years.

Wanda outlined the weekend's events, concluding with a brief recounting of how they had become separated in the first place.

"Do you have any idea where to start?" Mona set a paper plate holding an untouched doughnut on the floor next to her chair. "Did she have an address book?"

"I haven't had a chance to go through all her things yet. I hadn't thought of that." Wanda realized she hadn't thought through the ways she could find Kendall.

"What about her friend—she couldn't tell you anything?" Yvette sat next to Wanda each time, although the two had never exchanged a word of conversation outside the group.

"No."

The group was silent for a moment. "So how are you handling all this?" Mona's euphemism for "Did you fall off the wagon?"

"I can't say I didn't want to buy out the liquor store for a while Saturday night. Goodness knows, I've tried doing it before."

Nods of agreement. "You have to put your mind where it's not tempted," Mona said. "Stay focused on your goals. Your AA goals and your personal goals."

Wanda stared into her empty coffee cup. "I've put it in God's hands. I'm hoping he will show me where to look."

"That might be a long wait," Yvette said. She had the reputation as the group naysayer, in spite of everyone's efforts to encourage optimism.

"Haven't you ever heard the expression 'seek and ye shall find'?" Mona watched her with a bemused expression.

"Every time I ever seeked, all I ever got was lost," Yvette shot back, breaking the tension. Wanda had to smile herself.

"I've been seeking something ever since I decided to stop drinking," Wanda said. "Now that I know what it is—or who it is—I just hope I can figure out how to find her."

AFTER THE MEETING, the group scattered, and Wanda went out to her car. She turned, surprised to find Yvette staring at her across the hood.

"Did you need something?" Oddly, Wanda felt a little afraid.

"I just wanted to say I know what it's like."

"What what's like?"

"To have somebody missing from your life. My problem is I never found the courage to go looking."

"I wouldn't call it courage. It's more of a need."

"Words, Wanda. It takes guts to look the past in the face." Yvette tapped on the hood. "You find your girl. I'm there in spirit."

"Thank you, Yvette," said Wanda, giving her a tentative smile. "That means a lot."

"Don't tell nobody. I done built up a reputation here."

"My lips are sealed."

Yvette grinned and walked away. Wanda got in her car and prepared herself for work. *If Yvette can get behind me, and God is already behind me, then what have I got to lose?* she thought, cranking the engine, hoping the old car would take her wherever she needed to go to find the daughter she loved more now than she ever had before.

five

EACH NIGHT WANDA RUSHED HOME to go through the boxes. Some contained only kitchen items—silverware or drinking glasses or baking paraphernalia. Others held wads of soft clothing carelessly packed. These Wanda washed and ironed and hung in the closet in the guest bedroom, but not before inhaling them to see if they smelled of her daughter—not that she really knew what that was. Perfume perhaps? How could she remember what Kendall's scent was, what with being saturated by the smell of beer or whatever her flavor of the month was.

As she sorted the contents of one box after another, she prayed for God to show her how to find her child. But the farther she dug, the more confused she became. Why would anyone leave all these good memories behind? Kendall obviously had them. Lists of people for whom she baked cookies, cakes, and pies, apparently the beginning of a client list for that catering business Christine Davenport had mentioned. A collection of cookbooks and recipes carefully transcribed onto recipe cards hand-decorated with drawings of chickens and fruit and vegetables.

Then she discovered the box with the journals.

Kendall's journals formed a teetering stack nearly two feet tall. Written in spiral notebooks earlier, hardbound books covered with floral fabrics later, they chronicled her growth from an angry, resentful teenager to a young woman filled with ambition, caring, and a great capacity for forgiveness.

In her day, Wanda had called them diaries. She had never kept one herself, but she knew childhood friends who had. Writing down her daily activities or exploring her feelings had never seemed important to her. The drunken rampages of her own parents had scarred her own childhood. She felt ashamed that she had exposed Kendall to the same types of outbursts she had so dreaded and deplored as a child. As she got older, though, she found herself taking little sips from the glasses her parents left around the house and grew to crave the sensations it gave her—and took away. The pain disappeared when she drank. So she continued, drinking more and more and more until she didn't have any feelings of her own, just the ones that flowed from those seemingly magic liquids that eventually took over her life.

Wanda noted the clearly marked dates on the first page of each journal until she found the first entry, one written many years before. At first she wondered if she should read the journals at all. Suppose Kendall came back and found out that her mother had read all of her private thoughts? How could her daughter ever trust her? Wanda piled the books on the dining table and watched them for several days, as if waiting for Kendall herself to pop from the neatly handwritten pages like a genie from a bottle, reading the words in person.

Finally, she couldn't stand it anymore. Kendall was missing, and Wanda had to find her. The first step would be to learn who her daughter was by reading her own words.

When she opened the first journal, a blue spiral notebook covered with the names of songs and rock groups, the titles slanted to form a diamond pattern across the covers, she found her palms were damp. She began reading:

I left home today. I never thought I'd get the courage to leave the drunk, but today I just packed my bags and walked. Rochelle's letting me stay here for a few days, but I don't know how long her mom is going to go for that. My job at the burger joint doesn't pay enough for me to get my own place. I guess I didn't think this out well, but I am NOT going back!!! She has hurt me for the last time. I'm too young to be cleaning up after my own mother. She doesn't care where she gets sick, and I have to be the one to take care of it. I want to be free. Free from her. Free from being responsible for her. Free from her jerky boyfriends who are always putting their paws all over me, like I'm some kind of bonus prize to "her man." She doesn't even know I'm there half the time, and when she does, all she does is order me around.

I am never going back to her. If she loves that bottle more than she loves me, the bottle can have her. I'll make my way somehow.

Wanda closed the notebook and lay her head down on the table.

"Dear God," she implored, "why did I do this to my own child? How can she ever forgive me?"

Someone knocked at the door. She sat up and dried her eyes. A quick look in the hall mirror reflected the face of grief, and it was a face she knew she couldn't hide. She opened the door to find Mel, holding a basket of fruit.

"Thought you might like something less Floridian," he said, entering without invitation and placing the basket of apples and pears on the table. "We're citrused to death down here."

Wanda found herself laughing through her tears. "Thank you, Mel. If an apple a day keeps the doctor away, I had better eat that whole basket right now!"

Mel smiled and sat. "We've been missing you at the meetings. Figured I better come and check on you what with this business with your daughter and all."

Wanda nodded. "I've been so preoccupied that I've only been to one meeting since I came back."

"You can't let yourself get off track now. Especially now." He patted her hand. "You're very vulnerable, and that's when the temptation to drink is the strongest."

41

"If you read what I just read you would never even want another drink." She opened the journal and pushed it toward Mel, who read silently.

"Strong words. How old was she when she wrote this?"

"Sixteen," Wanda said, closing the book again. "As nearly as I can recall."

"You gotta remember, though, a lot of kids hate their moms at that age."

"Only problem is, most moms aren't as hateful as I was." Wanda went into the kitchen and began making coffee. "I gave her plenty of good reasons to write that."

Mel sat back in his chair. "Got any new ideas on how you're going to find her?"

Wanda pulled out a yellow legal pad. "I jotted down a few ideas, but I don't know what I'm doing. I'm not a detective. If the police would help . . ."

"They won't? They're supposed to. That's what they're there for."

"She's an adult. They all seem to think she took off of her own free will."

"You don't think she did?"

"Not from what I've learned." She recounted her meetings with Oscar Davenport, George Pettit, and Mandy. "She is not the kind of person who would just up and leave everything." Wanda winced at the thought, knowing that her daughter had left her. "I've been going through her things, and she's not at all like me. She's responsible and caring. She went to work on time, and baked cookies for people, and she was planning to start her own business." She returned to the kitchen and poured the coffee. She served the steaming mug to Mel, and they threaded their way to the living room sofa.

"Have you tried contacting the media?" Mel asked before carefully sipping the dark brew.

"Oh, heavens. There is no way I could ever talk to a TV reporter!" Wanda shivered. "I can barely get up at a meeting and tell how I became such a lush. If I went on TV I'd have to explain too much, and I'm not prepared to embarrass Kendall by doing that, if she is where she can see it."

"Then what kind of ideas do you have?"

Wanda flipped to the handwritten list. "I can put up flyers around towns in Florida between here and where Kendall lived. Lives, I mean," she corrected, irritated with herself for using the past tense. "Mandy offered to help me. She even gave me a photo of Kendall. Would you like to see it?" She didn't wait for an answer, going into the bedroom to retrieve her purse.

"She's a beautiful girl," Mel said when she returned holding the photo in front of her like a prized plaque. "She has your eyes. A lot of resemblance there."

"I think maybe there would be more if I had taken better care of myself," Wanda replied ruefully, taking the picture back and balancing it on her knees.

"So any other suggestions? For finding Kendall, I mean." Mel leaned forward with interest.

"I can trace the route she would have taken to come back here."

"And do what? She could be anywhere."

Wanda sighed. "Check the hospitals, sheriffs' departments? I don't know, Mel, but I have to try something."

"That's gonna take so much time, Wanda."

"After all these years, I'm willing to take however much time I have to. She's my girl, and I know she's in trouble. For so many years, I lost the connection I had with her, and now I feel it; I feel it in my heart. I have to look for her."

"Wanda, whatever you need, I'm willing to help. I didn't mean to criticize." She was heartened by the warm look in his eyes. "I'm just concerned about you. I have kids myself, up north, and I don't know what I'd do if one of 'em ever went missing." He glanced at his watch. "I didn't realize it was getting so late. I'm probably keeping you from your bedtime."

"Hardly. I've been having trouble sleeping."

Mel rose and turned to face her. "I hope that doesn't mean you're looking for a way to get yourself a good night's rest."

Wanda shook her head. "I'd be lying if I said I wasn't tempted. But I have something important to do. I hope this doesn't sound hokey, but I feel like God is leading me and giving me strength in a way I never felt before. Like I'm just now achieving my true sobriety."

Mel smiled. "It takes a while, Wanda. I've been watching you all this time, watching your progress. You're doing well, but you need to keep up with the meetings." He playfully wagged a finger in her face.

"I know, and I'll be there Friday night," she said. "Thanks for coming by, Mel. It means a lot that you care."

Wanda watched as he got into his car and drove away, staying on the stoop to enjoy the cool night air. She looked up at the stars, wondering how God, who created such a massive, majestic universe, could take the time to care so much about his messed-up children, children like herself. She had never thought of God as a father figure until she became a Christian. In fact, her knowledge of God before that was nearly non-existent. Her parents had never taken her to church, and she only knew of Jesus as a little baby in the manger scenes that popped up in department store windows at Christmastime.

Each day now, though, she understood more about God's mercy, how he loves and disciplines his children. How much she had to learn from him about dealing with her own child, although Kendall was grown and their relationship was tenuous at best.

She drank in the stars before going inside, thinking that if God could find a way to hear her prayer out of the millions he heard every second, maybe he could make time to give an answer to hers. If only it could be the answer she wanted to hear.

"I REACHED A POINT where I wanted to stop living a life that I was ashamed of." Wanda stood before the coed AA group, her hands folded, recounting the moment when she decided to stop drinking.

"I had to do it, first for myself. I can't say I lost any respect for myself, because if I had any self-respect to begin with, I wouldn't have become an alcoholic. I never would have even started drinking."

She paused and looked around the room. Mel sat in the back, nodding with silent encouragement.

"I wanted to be accepted, but most of all I wanted to be loved. When I was drinking, I felt lovable. I was different when I was drinking, someone outgoing and fun-loving. When I wasn't drinking, I was hateful and angry." Many in the room nodded. Wanda ran her hands over the smooth wood of the podium, collecting her thoughts.

"I've been trying to follow the program, do everything I'm supposed to do. I'm to the point of making amends, and as many of you know, that means I've been trying to find my daughter, Kendall. She's my only child, and she left home when she was sixteen because of my drinking. I've had little contact with her since then.

"When I went to see her, I found out she had disappeared. No letter or forwarding address, nothing. She left behind her job, her clothes, everything. Even her friends." She stopped and took a deep breath. "Her best friend said Kendall may have been on her way to see me. And she just disappeared."

Leaving the podium, she came and stood in the narrow aisle that divided the rows of chairs. "I am about to take a journey, and it might even be more important than the one I took to get sober. I'm going to search for my daughter. I think someone took Kendall, and it's going to be up to me to get her back.

"I believe in God and that he gives us all the capacity to forgive. Without preaching to you, I learned a verse in church, that Jesus taught that we should forgive seventy times seven. From what I've been able to find out about Kendall, I hope that she has found it in her heart to forgive me now for everything I did to her. I just have to find her."

Wanda sat back down and closed her eyes, feeling a sudden sense of exhaustion. Speaking to a group was very trying for her, but she knew she needed to develop her confidence

45

if she hoped to question everyone she needed to so she could find her child.

A few other members of the group told their stories before the group broke up for the evening. Some gathered around the coffeepot, catching up on non-group issues, while Wanda and Mel walked to the parking lot.

"So have you mapped your strategy yet?" Mel dug his hands in his pockets and leaned against the hood of Wanda's car. A cool breeze flowed across the lot as the stars winked into view.

"Mapped? You wouldn't believe." Maps of Florida, Georgia, and South Carolina that she had ordered through tourism bureaus, auto clubs, and chambers of commerce covered her dining room table. At the library, she had compiled an extensive list of police and sheriffs' departments, complete with addresses and telephone and fax numbers—hospitals, too. Mandy had designed a flyer with Kendall's photo, name, vital statistics, and the circumstances of her disappearance, and they had spent an afternoon making stacks of copies at a quick print shop located in a strip mall. Wanda hadn't taken a vacation in two years and had four weeks of vacation time coming. Her manager had agreed to let her take all the time at once in January, when business was slow and he could get by without her help.

"So when are you leaving?"

"The day after New Year's," Wanda replied.

"I wish I could do something to help you."

The kindness in Mel's eyes was the boost Wanda needed. "I know. This is something I have to do myself. You know how that is." Mel had been a member of AA for more than twenty years. His years of sobriety were an inspiration to Wanda, and his friendship was now growing into a blessing she hadn't expected.

Mel nodded. "I care about you, and I don't want to see you get hurt. You're like one of my own kids."

"A kid at fifty. Who'd have imagined that?" She laughed and playfully punched his arm. "What's hurting me is not knowing where Kendall is, if she's okay, if she's not okay. I have to do this, and I have to do it now."

Mel took her hand in his and squeezed it tightly. "If you need me to do anything back here, anything at all, you call me."

"I will, Mel. You're a good friend," she said. *I wish my father had been as supportive as you.*

"I'm just trying to do my part."

"I'll call you before I go."

"If I don't call you first."

Wanda got into her car and drove away, glad that although she would be making this journey by herself, she wouldn't be making it alone.

Along I-95,
Northern Florida

THE EMPLOYEES of Clay Manufacturing jumped enthusiastically into their litter clean-up project. It was the last one scheduled this year for their assigned stretch of road.

As they approached a wooded area, one woman spotted a suitcase. Alerting her coworkers, they went to investigate. The bag had no identification tag and was full of women's clothing, shoes, and toiletries.

"Probably fell off the top of somebody's SUV," one said.

"Then how did it get way over here?" another asked.

"Bounced," said one guy, who went on ahead.

"Well, what should we do with it? It's too heavy to carry in a trash bag, and these clothes are really nice."

The trash collection truck, hauling a trailer into which they tossed their filled bags, pulled alongside. The woman who found the suitcase ran over and chatted briefly with the driver.

"He says he can take it to the Goodwill store, and they can sell the bag and its contents. Just put it in the bed of the truck."

One of the men picked it up and threw it easily into the vehicle.

"I hope she had something to wear when she got where she was going," the woman said.

"I guess she probably had to buy all new things," her coworker replied, sighing. "Every woman's dream—start all over with a brand-new wardrobe. I just hope she didn't lose her credit cards, too."

six

THE MECHANIC TINKERED under the hood, pulling hoses and checking connections. Wanda watched from the office, barely able to see him through a window plastered with greasy handprints. After several anxious moments he came in, wiping his hands on a bright orange rag.

"You're going to have to leave it, ma'am."

Wanda planned to begin her search for Kendall in a few days. But this morning when she had turned the ignition of her car, all she had gotten in return was a grinding sound followed by a deafening silence.

"What's wrong with it?"

The mechanic scratched his head. "I'm not quite sure yet. I may have to consult with my colleagues," he replied with a grin, sounding as much like a doctor as an auto repairman. *Might as well be one as the other*, Wanda thought. *Both charge a mint.* She had already paid an exorbitant towing fee, and she could hear the distinctive ring of a cash register in her mind.

First the landlord decided to raise the rent, starting immediately, and now her main means of transportation was shot. "How long do you think it'll be?"

"Probably next week."

"Next week!" Wanda shook her head. "I need it back today."

49

"I might have to order parts. It's a holiday weekend coming up, what with New Year's and all. We're going to be closed part of that time."

Her heart sank. No one ever expects their car to break down, even if it is an old one, and she hadn't budgeted for this. She had concentrated on saving every spare dime to put toward her trip, and that was with plans to stay in budget motels and eat fast-food specials at interstate interchanges along the way. Time was a factor, too. What she really needed was eight-day weeks and thirty-six-hour days to accomplish all she needed to do. She didn't know how long or how detailed her search would be. Nevertheless, she knew she couldn't afford to lose another day.

Now she had no choice. It was either have the car repaired or rent one, and she couldn't afford to rent a car for an entire month.

"Do whatever you have to do," she said, resigning herself to the situation. Becoming angry or impatient wouldn't get the car fixed any faster. "Can I use your phone to call a friend?"

"There's a pay phone out front."

Wanda turned away without a word. *Charge you all that money and won't let you make one measly phone call?* She went outside and called Lottie, who promised to be there within the half hour.

She sat on a bench and watched the traffic whisking by on the busy city street. Earlier, she had called her boss from home and explained the situation, and he allowed her to take the morning off. More money lost.

The sky became overcast, and the neon light on a bar across the street blinked at Wanda, casting a come-hither look that she ignored. It was before noon, but time has no meaning to an alcoholic. Back when she drank, she found that any hour could become happy hour with just a few sips of distilled emotion, poured straight up. She closed her eyes so she couldn't see the people going in and out, the ones going in walking straight, the ones coming out walking slightly slanted.

There but for the grace of God go I, she thought, going to the soda machine for a Sprite. When the can clinked into the dispenser, she turned to find Lottie waiting inside her little red sports car. Wanda eased through the door.

"I think it'd be easier to crawl into this thing," she said, finally settling in and fastening her seat belt.

Lottie laughed and pulled into traffic. "I always wanted a hot car, and when I finally was able to afford one, you couldn't hold me back," she said. Wanda was always relieved, however, that Lottie's flamboyant style didn't carry over into her driving. In fact, she drove the car more like it was made out of pure crystal than fiberglass, metal, and rubber.

They rode silently toward the shopping center where Wanda worked. "I take it this puts a hitch in your plans," said Lottie, slowing to catch a red light.

"I don't know when I'll be able to leave now."

Lottie tapped the steering wheel in time with the country music that danced from the speakers. "You know, maybe this is the Lord's way of telling you it's not time yet."

"What do you mean? I have to find her. She could be in real trouble."

The light changed, and Lottie accelerated cautiously. "I'm saying that maybe you need to slow down and rethink this plan of yours a little bit. I mean it's really hit and miss."

Wanda fought a desire to jump out of the car. "Well, if you have any suggestions that you've been holding back, I wish you'd tell me now. I've been asking you for weeks if you know of a better way, and now you're telling me I'm going off on a wild-goose chase."

"Calm down, hon. I don't mean that at all. I'm just saying that maybe you need to approach this in a little more organized way."

"How do you suggest I do that? I don't know where Kendall was going when she left her house. Maybe she wasn't coming to see me. Maybe she *was* going to meet some man." She looked at the leftover Christmas decorations that dotted the city streets. Where before they had looked cheerful and bright, they now sagged beneath the burden of seasonal expectations. "I don't know, Lottie. I want to find her so badly. I just want to see her again."

"Did you ever find out anything from those journals of hers?"

"I've barely touched them. I read a few passages in the first one. She was so full of anger and hatred, all of it directed straight at me, and I can tell you, I deserved every line of what she wrote." She cringed at the memory of Kendall's caustic words. "I can't bring myself to read them again." She thought of the stack still standing on the dining table.

"Then what you need to do is start now and work back."

"Start now?"

"Start with the more recent ones. Find out what she was thinking and doing before she disappeared. Who she was doing it with, hon. There's your clues right there."

The car rolled to a stop in front of the mall. "I'm sorry I got mad at you. It's all just too hard for me to face."

"You'll face it. You've got me and Mandy and Mel. We're all standing right here with you." Lottie patted her arm. "Now you go home tonight and read those books again. I bet there's something in there you hadn't even thought of."

"Maybe you're right." Wanda turned to get out. "And you might think of putting some kind of handle on top of this door over here."

"Why is that?"

"To help people get out. Like I said before . . ."

". . . it'd be easier to fall out and then stand up," they finished in unison.

Wanda smoothed her hair and walked to her job, wondering why all of her answers in life seemed to come from somewhere—or someone—else.

This guy living next door to me has some real problems. I hear him through the wall at night, talking out loud. It's not like he's talking to anyone specifically either, like he's not even

52

talking on the phone. I'm sure he's not talking to the television. I don't believe he even owns one.

Wanda sipped a cup of decaf as she read the most recent journal. It did not contain entries for the days just before her disappearance, leading her to believe Kendall must have started another book and taken it with her. Yet this account was vastly different from the first book. The adult Kendall had a wonderful maturity and curiosity about life that the adolescent Kendall had buried beneath resentment and anger.

I cooked supper for him a few times and gave it to him through the door. I think he's out of work right now. At least he doesn't seem to be leaving the house during the day. Sometimes he goes out at night for an hour or two, then he comes home and starts all that talking. I'd like to ask him if he's talked to anyone, I mean like a counselor or psychiatrist or something like that, but I wouldn't want to offend him. I'd really like to help him, but I don't know how.

The man's name was noticeably absent. Flipping the pages and skimming, Wanda could find no trace. He was always just "the guy next door." She wished she had taken the time to ask Mandy or Oscar Davenport who the man was. Reading on, she found several more references to him. Apparently Kendall had become more concerned about her neighbor's behavior but was at a loss as to what to do about it.

I'd talk to Mr. Davenport about him, but I'm afraid I'd get him evicted, and I hate to see anyone homeless. I've been there, and it's not a good place.

Wanda winced at the memory. Shelters were terrible places for adults, much less children. It had taken a very long time to forgive herself for placing Kendall in that position, so she understood her daughter's compassion.

He must be receiving disability payments; otherwise I don't know how he would pay the rent and utilities. He's obviously mentally ill. If anyone has ever been to visit him, I haven't seen them. I wish I knew what to do.

The journals went on similarly, until Wanda reached an entry that caused her to catch her breath.

I heard from Daddy today. He tracked me down by phone and asked me to come and visit him. He said his work keeps him very busy or he would have come to see me by now. It's been so long. I barely remember him. At least the memories I have of him are more pleasant than the ones I have of Mom.

The words wavered beneath Wanda's stare. Kendall had talked with Derek.

Derek had been her first husband. She had married again, a fellow drunk who stayed with her until he saw he might have to get out and work to support them; then he left for parts unknown.

Derek was different. He had loved her. And she had been too messed up to accept his love or to return it.

So it came as a blow that after all these years he had acknowledged his daughter's existence and that Kendall had accepted him back into her life so easily.

Her stomach churned. Derek had abandoned them—why could Kendall forgive him so easily, yet forget that she had another parent who also needed forgiveness? She couldn't understand.

She snapped the journal shut and threw it on the pile, which swayed and toppled to the floor. Wanda didn't bother picking up the mess; instead she picked up her purse. Perhaps Lottie had been right. It wasn't time yet to look for her daughter. Right now it was time to look for an all-night bar, a place where she was sure of one thing—all it took to be accepted was a few bucks and a stiff chaser.

seven

KING'S GRANT, SOUTH CAROLINA

IT HAD ALREADY BEEN A LONG DAY, and judging from the insistent pager vibrating against Bruce Yeats's waist, it was about to get longer. He stared at the back door, preparing to knock when Janelle opened it and stared back. They regarded each other for a moment before she pushed open the screen.

"You're too late. Daniel already took off with his friends." She turned and walked into the kitchen. Bruce let the door slam shut behind him.

"You could have told him to wait," Bruce said, trying to switch off the pager before she turned around. "I got held up."

"By one of those crooks you're always chasing?" She kept walking into the family room, a misnomer now if ever there was one. It had been a while since they had all done anything as a family. Sometimes Bruce wondered if they had ever really been one.

Finally Janelle turned to face him. Her words stung like wind-driven sleet. He didn't respond.

"He looks up to you, you know. His dad, the tough cop, the hard-edged detective. Are you aware he keeps a scrapbook about every case you've ever handled?"

Bruce looked away. The pager kept nudging him. *Not now,* he thought. *Always at the worst times.* "I never knew that," he said, his voice quiet. "I want to do better."

"If you wanted to do better, you would have done it by now." Janelle sat in the recliner and rocked until Bruce thought the chair would launch itself through the ceiling. Bruce tried to meet her eyes, but she stared at the last of November's scarlet leaves cascading past the picture window.

When he and Janelle had married eighteen years before, Bruce felt he had married for life. He and Janelle had so much in common. They liked the same movies and books, and they shared a love for the outdoors, the active life of skiing and hiking through the Blue Ridge Mountains just a few hours away. They envisioned life as an adventure, full of places and experiences to explore and enjoy. As a couple they longed for a son, and Daniel had come along sooner than they planned. They deemed it a sign that they must be ready for parenthood, and so they doted on the boy. Although Bruce was an only child and wanted more children to keep his son from the loneliness he had felt growing up, Janelle had come from a large family and felt she had spent enough time raising her younger brothers and sisters. One was enough for her, and whatever Janelle wanted, Bruce gave her.

Their happiness, their joy—somehow it had slipped away, given way to the drudgery of everyday life. Jobs, careers—Bruce's especially. As a sheriff's investigator, he learned the job never entailed a nine-to-five shift. He was on call, 24-7-365. He couldn't even say he had a real day off during a leap year.

It wasn't just the hours, though. It was the nature of the job. On the one hand, he felt as if he were truly helping people by getting criminals off the streets, at least temporarily. Sometimes it seemed as if he was fighting a losing battle. Arrested by midnight, out on bail the next morning. The constant exposure to humanity's baser elements had affected Bruce's psyche in ways he hadn't fully comprehended. Growing cynicism. A short temper. Impatience with any type of bad behavior on Daniel's part. Although Bruce was rarely around, he had grown to be a strict disciplinarian. Sometimes he felt as if that man wasn't him. Only he couldn't remember who the real Bruce Yeats was.

It was the same with Janelle. She was a nurse, and the hospital was constantly calling her to work the night shift to fill in for staff shortages, much as Bruce did for the understaffed sheriff's department. She, too, had become sardonic, bitter, hating her job but not willing to give it up for something she might enjoy more.

It was no way to keep a marriage together. They passed each other in doorways, barely seeing one another physically, much less taking the time even to ask about the other's day. As time passed, each demanded change from the other without a willingness to make a break with their own problems. They had grown apart, slowly, then in spurts, until the day came when Janelle asked him—no, *told* him—to move out, saying they had no future left, at least with each other.

"I want to come home so we can try and work things out," he said, putting himself between his wife and the view.

"If we couldn't work things out when you were home before, and we can't work them out now, what makes you think that your coming back is going to make working out our problems any easier? What will that do to Daniel?"

At sixteen, Daniel had become a handful. A good kid before the separation, his grades had begun to slip, and the calls from the principal about his behavior—fights, talking back, making threats to other students—had become far too frequent. He had been left to raise himself too early. Bruce had seen it often: latchkey kids who rebelled against their parents' absences by doing the only thing left to get attention—find trouble. In spite of all the strict punishments and restrictions, his son was now doing the same thing, something Bruce couldn't have imagined the first time he held his cooing baby in his arms. This separation was taking its toll on all three of them. Bruce put his hand on the pager without thinking.

"Don't ignore it on account of me." Janelle picked up a magazine and flipped through it, barely looking at the pages.

"Someone else can handle it," Bruce said. "We need to talk."

"I don't have anything to say to you. If you can't clear a day off to spend time with your son, then what can I do about it? You *won't* do anything."

"It's not like I *can* do anything. You knew that when you married me. This job—it's all I know how to do. It's what makes me happy, Janelle."

"It's good to know something does."

"Are you sure you aren't jealous?"

She finally looked at him, incredulous. "Jealous? You're calling me jealous? Of your job?"

"That I like it. Can you say that about working in the ICU?"

Janelle flipped her hair from her shoulders. In another time, Bruce would have found the gesture appealing. Now he found it defiant. "Let me tell you something. I help people, too. I may not get out there and play the hero, but I make a difference to people. It's just a shame that I can't seem to make a difference to you."

The pager vibrated again. Bruce cursed and snatched it from his waistband.

"Duty calls, as usual."

"You don't have to be like this, Janelle."

"Then how should I be?" She finally looked at him, and it wasn't anger that he saw in her expression. It was sadness. Maybe not even that. Disappointment.

He sighed and turned to leave. "Tell Daniel I'll call him. We'll set another time."

"I'll tell him not to hold his breath."

"Don't put him in the middle of this."

"It's too late," she said, going into the bedroom, leaving Bruce alone and feeling like a stranger not only in his own house but in his own life.

THE RESPONDING DEPUTIES had cordoned off an area about sixty feet square with yellow police tape by the time Bruce arrived. He pulled his unmarked sedan into a vacant spot near the coroner's van. Two deputies, Jason Kiley and Trey Burns, came over and filled him in as they walked to the restricted area.

"McGarrity's having a cow about you not being here," Jason said as they picked their way through the vines that covered the forest floor. "He's been paging you forever."

"I had some personal business." Bruce resented the young man's conveyance of his boss's irascibility. Patience had never been Sheriff Marty McGarrity's strong suit. "Tell me what we got here."

Trey pointed to the center of the clearing. "A hiker found a body. At least they think it's a body. Ain't much left, 'cept some bones sticking out from under a pile of leaves."

"Where's the hiker?"

Jason pointed to a man seated on the running board of a bystander's red pickup truck, smoking a cigarette. "Says he was making a scouting trip for a hunting excursion he had planned for this weekend."

"Make sure he sticks around. I'll need to ask him some questions."

Bruce ducked under the tape. The coroner, Morris Lund, walked around the perimeter to greet him. "It looks bad, Bruce."

"You look at it up close yet?"

"Close enough to know we got a lot of work to do."

Bruce examined the ground carefully, his hands balled into fists in his jacket pockets, mindful that they could be treading over potential evidence that could be useful later. He scanned the corpse.

"No clothes?" He reached into Morris's open crime kit and retrieved a pair of latex gloves.

"None that we've recovered," Morris said, hunkering down. "No personal effects, except a pearl pendant—pretty generic."

He peered at the head. "From what hair's left, I think we might be dealing with a woman's body, but I can't even be sure of that."

"Did you call the pathologist?"

"Yeah. I'm going to take the body over there when we finish. The autopsy'll tell us a lot."

Morris left Bruce alone with the body. He walked around it carefully, taking photographs and notes, noting the body's position—its orientation facing east—as if it had been placed that way deliberately. He remembered something his mother once told him about how bodies are buried facing east, so they will be facing the direction of Christ's return. *A lot of bunk*, he had thought, the same thought he entertained when dealing with almost anything related to God or religion, be it Baptist or Buddhist. When he finished taking the first round of pictures, he swept off the leaves and brown pine needles that had been piling up on the remains, probably just in the last few days as they had begun falling in earnest. The rising wind from an approaching cold front blew them back as quickly as Bruce brushed them away.

Bruce's job included not only investigating burglaries, armed robberies, and assaults, it also involved looking into suspicious deaths. During his twenty years in law enforcement, he had seen his share of violent crime—women shot by deranged, abusive husbands; drug deals gone bad, ending in drive-by shootings; convenience store robberies turned uglier with the introduction of a stolen pistol.

This was the first time he had ever seen anything like this, though, something anyone involved in policing hoped never to see. A dead body bearing no immediate means of identification.

Surely it was a missing person from another county. Bruce could think of no outstanding missing person reports from King's Grant. He made a mental note to double-check when he got back to the office.

"Any first impressions?" Morris stood next to Bruce, sucking a grape lollipop. The coroner's fondness for lollipops and his balding head had earned him his rightful nickname.

"You know the rules, Kojak. No food or drink in the dead zone." Gallows humor was Bruce's way of dealing with situations he couldn't face otherwise. Even the toughest cop had to have a little built-in defense mechanism.

"This isn't food. It's nutritional enhancement. Sugar's a well-known preservative, you know." Morris finished the candy, then wrapped the stick in tissue and placed it in his pocket. He gestured toward the body. "I think it's a female. Other than that, we'll have to wait on the autopsy results." A shadow crossed his face. "Something about this look familiar to you?"

"Yeah," Bruce replied. "Way too familiar."

"You been to see her lately?"

"No. I keep in touch by phone though. The nurses give me updates."

"Any change?"

"Not that they've mentioned."

Bruce stood back, remembering the last visit to the nursing home.

NURSES MOVED EFFICIENTLY around the bed, adjusting tubes and checking monitors that beeped throughout the day and night, marking each respiration and heartbeat.

She had been there since early summer, another young woman without a name. Found in a wooded area by some hikers, she was barely alive then, barely alive now. Yet the nurses and doctors had grown to love her, the woman known only as Jane Doe. They loved her for her fighting spirit, for her will to live despite the horrors she had endured at the hands of a lunatic.

Her eyes would not open, though, and no one knew if they would ever see again, not just in the literal sense, but see the world the way the woman had seen it before. They didn't know which memories she would recall, although they all secretly hoped that she would not recall how she had come to be here but that she would remember the name of the one who had done this crime, so he could be punished, by man's justice, by God's justice.

61

Each day they watched for signs of renewed life—the flicker of an eyelid, the twitch of a finger or a toe, her first words, as if she were an infant about to speak for the first time.

Each day they waited for someone to come, to claim this young woman as a daughter, a wife, a sister.

No one came.

So they kept waiting, tending to her needs, until someone did decide to care, and perhaps they would be the one to see that twitch or feel the first grasp of her weakened hand.

MORRIS WAVED TO THE DEPUTIES who brought over a long black bag. They all worked together to move the remains, a painstaking task. Bruce noticed that Jason looked a little green.

"This your first dead body?"

"No, sir. Just my first skeleton."

"Believe it or not, it's my first skeleton, too." Bruce stood back as Morris zipped up the bag, and they all carried it to the white van parked on the shoulder of the road. Bruce spoke quietly to Jason. "Take our witness on down to the station. I'll question him there." A small crowd of onlookers had gathered, as had reporters from the three local television stations, and Bruce didn't want the man to feel intimidated. Kelly Karlisle from Channel 3 dodged the others and thrust a microphone under Bruce's nose as he extracted himself from the van.

"What can you tell us about the body you just removed from the woods?"

Bruce glanced at his watch. At 4:15, it was too early for Kelly to go live. "We have definitive proof now that Bigfoot exists. Three thousand miles out of his turf but dead and gone in the great state of South Carolina."

Kelly sighed and spun around, motioning the camera operator to cut. Bruce couldn't resist a smirk. Kelly turned back to find the van pulling away and Bruce walking toward his cruiser. She ran after him.

"Don't you have any comment at all?"

He noted that she had left the microphone behind, along with the camera man. The other reporters, apparently new to their jobs, were busy harassing the deputies for information. His eyes swept the length of her body. "That's quite a fetching outfit you have on."

"Fetching? What are we, living in the Victorian age? Little House on the Prairie?"

Bruce leaned against the car and folded his arms. Kelly had gone to work for the TV station about six months earlier, assigned to the criminal justice beat. Bruce had become her main liaison for information regarding crime news, which meant he saw her nearly every day. Since the separation from Janelle, he had found himself drawn to her youthful enthusiasm and cool, stylish attitude. Maybe a little too drawn.

"Call me old-fashioned," he said, opening the door and starting the engine.

Kelly put her hands on the ledge of the opened window. "Call *me* when you get some info? Call me first?"

"Don't I always?"

Bruce pulled away, driving to the county's law enforcement complex where he would write up his notes and begin the search for the dead person's identity. As he drove, he compared Kelly with Janelle. He supposed it was the age difference. Maybe it was just all the years he and Janelle had spent together. Nothing between them seemed fresh and exciting anymore. It was almost like they knew too much about each other.

He had to put that aside now, though. He had a dead body here. Someone out there knew something. Someone always did. He just had to find them.

eight

WITH HIS SCRUFFY APPEARANCE, the hiker looked more like a vagrant to Bruce, who had seen his share over the years. His hair was matted and dirt caked his clothes, leading Bruce to believe the man had probably been living in the woods, rather than just passing through.

"Would you like some coffee? We're famous for our dough-nuts, you know," Bruce said by way of making the man feel at ease.

The man stared back blankly before cracking a smile. "I'd appreciate that," he said, his voice hoarse.

Bruce left his office and returned shortly with a steaming cup and a paper towel piled with an assortment of crullers. The man launched into the stack as if it were a feast. Bruce pulled out a legal pad. "What was your name again?"

"Jonesy Jones," he replied with his mouth full. "My mama ain't had much imagination when it came to namin' young'uns. You can call me J. J."

Bruce nodded. "All right, J. J. So how did you come to find the body? Can you tell me what you were doing out there?"

"Hiking." He wiped his mouth on his sleeve and avoided Bruce's eyes.

"Going anywhere in particular?"

"No. Just out for a stroll."

Bruce leaned forward. "You know we're not going to throw you in jail just because you were sleeping in the woods. We can help you."

J. J. looked at the doughnut in his hand. "I ain't done nothing to nobody."

"I know, J. J. But we've got a problem here, and I need you to tell me everything you know. Now, how long have you been living out there?"

"About six months."

Bruce blinked, glad the man wasn't watching him. Approximately the same amount of time the body had been there. "Can you remember when you first started staying there?"

"I ain't got no home, but I still got my mind, detective. I lost everything—my wife, my job, my house, my kids. Didn't have nowheres else to go. So I went down yonder in the gully and built myself a shack out of some old limbs and trash I hauled over from the dump—it ain't that far away, you know, and you sure as heck don't want to live where I live when the wind's blowin' wrong and . . ."

"Was there anybody hanging around in the woods when you came there?"

"There's always somebody hanging around. Woods is the place where you either come to see or come to hide, and I tell you, there's more hiding than seeing out yonder."

"Well, while you were hiding, what did you see?"

"I seen a man bring a woman and lay her out all nice-like in that clearing."

Bruce stifled the urge to bang his fists on the desk. "J. J., if you saw him bring her there, why didn't you call somebody then? Why did you wait until now?"

J. J. finished the last doughnut and drank down the now-tepid coffee. "I had lawyers and bill collectors runnin' after me, not to mention my ex-wife wantin' every dime I ain't got. The woman was done dead. Weren't nothing nobody could do for her. The way I saw it she was restin' in peace, which was more'n I could say for myself." He avoided Bruce's eyes. "I guess

I finally got to thinkin' she might have a family, and they might want to bury her proper."

Bruce took a deep breath and continued. "Can you tell me what the man looked like?"

"Mangy, like me."

"Can you be a little more specific? Did you notice how tall he was or what color his eyes or hair were . . ."

"Listen here, that man was hauling a dead woman through the woods. I wasn't about to get up close and make his acquaintance."

"How close were you to him?"

"About a hundred feet, I reckon, near as I can recall. It was late in the evening, too, around sundown."

Bruce doodled on the legal pad before coming around the desk. He didn't have any evidence to connect the man to any crime. "J. J., we're going to get you a place to sleep tonight where you can get cleaned up. I want you to think really hard and see if you can remember anything else between now and tomorrow, because we're going to talk again."

"You ain't gonna go back on your promise not to put me in jail, is you?" J. J. stood slowly and looked at Bruce out of the corner of his eye.

"If you can tell me something that will help me figure out who that woman is and who did this to her, then I might be inclined to cut you some slack." Bruce opened his office door, grateful for the fresh air that whooshed in. "Trey, take Mr. Jones here down to the men's shelter and see if they can keep him tonight." He pulled Trey to one side. "And make sure you keep an eye on him. I don't want him running off before I get a chance to talk to him some more," he added quietly before returning to his office and opening the window.

AT NOON THE NEXT DAY, Bruce sat at the computer, his eyes bleary from looking at page after page of missing person reports. He hadn't received the results of the autopsy yet, so he didn't really even know who he was dealing with here. Nevertheless, he decided to go ahead and start looking statewide, so they could match any potential missings with their Jane Doe.

That morning, he had gone back out to the site with the deputies, and they had performed a grid search for anything they might have missed the day before. They found nothing, except a few pieces of trash that could have blown there from the road nearby or been thrown down by careless hunters or campers. The area was a popular recreational spot—how the body had gone undetected for so long eluded Bruce's comprehension. He guessed King's Grant had become like so many other places. Home, but not a spot to stick around on the weekends. The mountains, the beach, the interstate called everyone to the open road, to pleasures far beyond anything their little town had to offer.

Jonesy Jones was his best lead, his only source of information at this point. Bruce had composed a lengthy list of follow-up questions for the meeting he had scheduled for that afternoon. It never ceased to amaze him how one human being could be so indifferent toward another, not just in the taking of life, but in his refusal to get involved.

Just then a noise caught his attention, and Bruce realized it was the bell of the First Baptist Church marking the end of Sunday services. *So much for a day of rest,* he thought, trying to remember the last time he'd had a Sunday off and knowing he wouldn't have wasted it on going to church, listening to some preacher telling him about the evils of the world. He knew all about it firsthand and figured he could preach a decent sermon or two himself, although it wouldn't necessarily be what the congregation might want to hear. Forgiveness and grace did not exist in his world, a world populated by worthless scum who have never heard of the Ten Commandments, much less regarded them as something they might need to obey. Bruce himself didn't put much stock in biblical edicts either. That was just another way of telling people what to do, when they ought to know in their own minds.

He dug through a stack of files, searching for the folder containing information regarding their hospitalized Jane Doe.

The more he thought about it, the more similar these cases seemed. He had just found the documents when a motion caught his eye.

"Got a minute?" Morris Lund leaned in the door, holding a thin file folder. "Preliminary autopsy report just came in."

Bruce motioned Lund to the chair in front of his desk. "What does it say?"

"A female, as I thought. Probably between the ages of eighteen and twenty-eight. About five feet, six inches tall, probably 120 to 150 pounds before she decomposed. Long, dark hair, maybe black or dark brown. The pathologist saved samples for DNA comparison. X-rays of her teeth, too."

"Any guess as to cause of death?"

"She had multiple fractures throughout her body. Probably enough to cause internal injuries."

"Like an accident or like a beating?"

"A beating, more than likely. The pathologist guesses the injuries could have caused enough damage for her to have bled to death."

Bruce shook his head. "Any evidence pointing to a weapon?"

Lund looked through the reading glasses he had recently acquired at the drugstore, the middle-aged man's first acquiescence to presbyopia. "The ubiquitous blunt instrument, my dear Holmes."

"Somewhere in America there's a dump full of all the blunt instruments linked to homicides throughout the country."

"If you find out where it is, let me and a few hundred other law enforcers know where it is. We got a bunch of unsolved crimes out here." He handed the file to Bruce. "Keep it. I made a copy."

Bruce flipped the pages. "How many unsolved murders do we have in King's Grant? Four?"

"By last count. All of them female, but none like this. We got suspects and identifications for two of the victims. Just haven't come up with enough evidence to pin the crimes down on anybody."

Leaning back in his chair, Bruce laced his hands together behind his head. "I hate loose ends. I'm thinking of asking McGarrity if we can start a cold case squad."

"A cold case squad in King's Grant? Based on four unsolved cases?" Lund laughed and pulled out a yellow lollipop. "You been watching *America's Most Wanted* again?"

"Of course. *Cops*, too, don't you know." Bruce smiled. These days, with such a mobile population, police and sheriff's departments needed all the help they could get. "You don't think McGarrity'll go for it, huh?"

Lund got up to leave. "We're understaffed as it is. You're pulling double shifts as it is. Even your own wife got fed up with the overtime." He winced and held up his hands. "Sorry. I didn't mean to tread on touchy ground."

Bruce waved him off. "It wasn't just the overtime. Things haven't been good for a while."

"Anytime you need to talk . . ."

"Thanks, man. I just need a break."

"Hey, don't we all. Catch you later."

Bruce turned his attention back to the report, comparing the photos he had taken with ones taken during the autopsy. If only the killer had left something besides a piece of jewelry that was probably sold in every chain store from King's Grant to Junalaska—a credit card, a grocery store discount card, something they could trace.

Yet they had found nothing. It was as if she had been placed there without hands, like she had fallen from the sky. But Bruce knew she hadn't. A man had put her there. An evil man that only Jonesy could identify.

"Any updates?" Kelly Karlisle stood in the doorway, her expression hopeful. "You're looking mighty serious."

"Mighty serious? You been parlayin' with them mountain folks agin'?" Bruce grinned and came around the desk.

"You know what I mean." She stood in front of Bruce while he surveyed her severe black suit.

"You going to a funeral or coming from one?"

She looked down at herself. "I'm doing a story on a murder investigation. I thought it would be fitting to dress conservatively, according to the mood of the story."

"Just who told you we had a murder investigation here?"

"A certain balding coroner."

Bruce smirked. "Don't let him hear you say that. He'll be subscribing to the Hair Club before we know it."

"Be serious now, Bruce. I need an update for the six o'clock broadcast. Come with me to the crime scene? Please?"

Sitting on the corner of the desk, he folded his arms. "Only if you'll go out to dinner with me after the news." He took a deep breath, surprised at himself but careful not to let it show.

"I don't know," she said, backing away. "Aren't you still married?"

"Separated. The only thing holding me and Janelle together is the absence of signatures on a piece of paper."

Kelly nodded. "I still don't know."

"Think about it."

"Maybe it would be better if you would just follow us in your car. I'll have to get right back to the station anyway."

Bruce stood and grabbed his keys from the desk drawer. "Anything you want, Kelly."

As he drove along behind the TV van, Bruce's thoughts drifted to Janelle, wondering what she was doing that night. Maybe she had started looking around, too. They hadn't lived together in months. When they separated, he had moved back home with his mother, who had raised him alone. Bruce hadn't seen his father since he was six. He often thought about his father and debated with himself whether he was worth searching for—after all, he had abandoned him and his mother. But Bruce kept putting off the search. He had more important cases.

Nearing the crime scene, he thought back on his Jane Does. Was anyone looking for them?

Bruce had seen many tragic scenes, but he had learned not to let separations between parents and children tear him apart. He knew what that hurt felt like, and he didn't want to feel it anymore. It had taken up too many years of his life.

When they arrived at the woods, Kelly and the camera operator set up while Bruce waited. He didn't walk back into the ravine, and he didn't invite Kelly to, either. It was still cordoned with yellow tape while he waited for the state's forensic investigators to sign off on the investigation. With an unidentified body, it was procedure to have the state people take a look and use whatever resources they had at their disposal to assist. When Kelly was ready, Bruce stepped up and answered her questions, leaving out details as usual so as not to compromise any information that might prove crucial to solving the murder. Those details to which only the killer and law enforcement would be privy. He didn't mention J. J. or the man he had seen, or the pendant, wanting to wait until he had a chance to question the vagrant further.

When they were finished, Bruce stepped back toward his cruiser. "Bruce?" He turned to find Kelly following him.

"I appreciate your invitation to dinner, but I'm not quite sure yet. Maybe another time?"

Bruce nodded and smiled. "Maybe so. Consider it an open invitation."

Kelly backed away, smiling as well. "I will."

Bruce donned his sunglasses against the glare brought on by the lower angle of the autumn sun. Maybe he had been too hasty in inviting Kelly out. He didn't know what he was thinking; after all, he didn't really know her. She had to have plenty of boyfriends at her age. Maybe he had been misreading her signals. Maybe he was paying too much heed to his own.

nine

MARINTHA YEATS THOUGHT the rich scent of cinna-mon must be the best the good Lord ever created. Scripture always mentioned spices, didn't it? She retrieved her tattered Bible from the nightstand and looked up cinnamon in the con-cordance. Flipping to Exodus, she found it was one of the main ingredients mixed with the oil used to anoint the Tent of Meet-ing. *That must have been one good-smelling place*, she thought as she put the Bible on the bed and returned to the kitchen, where the aroma of baking snickerdoodles filled the room.

Daniel was supposed to stop by after school to help her rake the pine straw that covered her yard. Bruce never seemed to have the time to help her with yard work anymore, although helping with the chores was to be a condition of his moving back home after the separation from Janelle. Yet instead of fuming over it, Marintha thought her grandson might need some spending money—it cost so much more now to be a teenager than it did when Bruce and Janelle were coming up.

She pulled on her oven mitts and retrieved the hot cook-ies from the oven, inhaling the fresh-baked scent as she trans-ferred them to a wire rack to cool. *Daniel should have been here by now*, she realized, checking the clock and seeing that it was almost four o'clock. Opening the front door, she stepped onto the porch of the old Craftsman-style house that she had inherited from her parents and scanned the street. Hardly anyone stayed home during the day now. The husbands and wives both worked. The children were packed off to daycare until they outgrew it, at which point they became latchkey kids or teenagers or both, with too much time and too little direction, getting into all sorts of devilment.

Going back inside, she called Janelle's house; no answer. She decided her daughter-in-law must be at work. She tried calling Bruce's direct line to his office but got a busy signal there. For all the ways to get in touch with people these days, it was getting harder and harder to communicate. Marintha had toyed with the thought of getting one of those home computers so she could e-mail everyone, like her friend, Etta. Etta was eighty years old and ran full blast on all eight cylinders. If she had half Etta's energy, Marintha thought, she could conquer sixteen fatal diseases and save half the unchurched population of the Southeast.

She sat at the table and watched the cooling cookies as if they might suddenly start marching away in their neat little rows. The front door slammed shut, and Daniel strode into the room.

"I was starting to get worried about you," Marintha said, rising to give her grandson a hug.

"No worries, Grammy," he replied, extracting himself from her arms and gathering a stack of cookies. "I had to meet a friend. Took a little longer than I thought."

"Oh, who is your friend?" Marintha always made it a point to ask Daniel specific questions whenever he came over. Bruce and Janelle's lack of knowledge of their own son's whereabouts and acquaintances appalled her. You could never be sure about anybody these days. "What's his name? Maybe I know his parents. Or his grandparents, more likely."

"I don't think so. A lot of new people live in King's Grant now. Even Mom and Dad can't keep up."

"I know," Marintha said, watching the cookies march their way down Daniel's throat into that hollow leg of his. Several new manufacturing plants had located to the area over the last decade, bringing an influx of transplants from all over the country. It was becoming harder to find a native-born South Carolinian anymore.

73

"Where's the rake?" Daniel had apparently finished snacking, leaving a lone row of cookies, which Bruce was certain to devour later.

"In the shed out back." Marintha told him where to put the raked leaves and pine straw, then watched him go at the job with the frenzied energy that only teenagers possess.

She went into the bedroom and held her Bible on her lap. Youth had always faced temptation but nothing like they did now. She thought about Bruce at Daniel's age. He had manifested the same frenetic energy, the same evasiveness—only the temptations had been tamer then. Crack cocaine, designer drugs, school shootings—none of these were a problem when Bruce was young. She feared for her grandson, and each day she prayed, placing him under the Lord's protection, just as she did Bruce for the dangerous situations he continually faced.

Marintha sat praying silently until she heard voices in the backyard. She looked out to see Bruce and Daniel wrestling in a newly raked mound of leaves. The sight pleased her greatly.

Bruce didn't spend nearly enough time with his son, even before the separation. Although Marintha had struggled to raise Bruce alone, sometimes working two or three jobs before she finally found the power company job, which brought her long-term security now that she was retired, she had always made time for her son. With two parents working, it seemed as if Daniel got short shrift all the way around. Despite Janelle's protests to the contrary, she never seemed to spend enough time with their son, either.

Maybe it was all this emphasis on consumption, keeping up with the neighbors. Bruce and Janelle had lived in an attractive house in a new neighborhood of middle-class houses. Marintha couldn't fault them for wanting to move up in the world. She had surely coveted that path often in her life, particularly when it seemed she wasn't going to have the money for the electric bill or to buy Bruce new school clothes. It was a different time now, and everything was aimed at getting bigger, better, faster, more. Mergers, acquisitions, expansions—the nightly news made Marintha's head spin.

She heard the back door open, and the boys—no matter how old they got, they would always be boys to her—came in laughing. Marintha lay down on the bed and pretended to take a nap. *They need some time alone,* she thought, enjoying the sound of laughter, wishing it could last until Bruce realized he needed to go home.

BRUCE AND DANIEL SAT at the kitchen table, drinking milk and dunking what was left of the cookies.

"So, any girls in the picture yet?" Bruce grinned slyly as he picked crumbs from his shirt.

"Dad! That's private!" Daniel blushed and looked out of the window.

"I see you turning purple over there. What's her name?"

"I don't want to talk about it yet."

"Yet." Bruce nodded. "So that means maybe you'll talk about it someday?"

Daniel regarded his father for a moment before answering. "Maybe. Depends how everything works out."

Bruce examined his son. The boy had taken on that midteen gangliness that afflicts adolescent boys, making them appear all arms and legs with only a slim box for a body to hold it together. His baggy clothes emphasized all this.

"You know, when I was in school, the tighter we could get our blue jeans, the better we liked it."

"Then you must have been fond of pain," Daniel retorted, snatching the last snickerdoodle. "Dad, why were you so late last Saturday?"

"Didn't you read the paper? Someone found a body in the woods. I'm the lead investigator." Bruce remembered Janelle's comment about Daniel's scrapbook. "Didn't you clip it out?"

"Oh, yeah," Daniel said vaguely. "I just haven't gotten around to reading the paper lately. Too much homework. You know how it is."

"Yeah, I know. It's going to take a lot of my time, at least for a while."

"That's okay. I know you're busy." Daniel looked pointedly at his watch. "Speaking of which, I gotta meet somebody."

"That girl?" Bruce asked, rising and following his son to the front door.

"You never know!" Daniel ran out and hopped into the used Toyota Bruce had given him for his birthday. He opened the window and shouted, "Say 'bye' to Grammy," waving before taking off much too rapidly down the deserted street.

"You should have pressed him more." Marintha's voice in the doorway startled Bruce.

"On what?"

"His friends. He claimed he had to meet somebody after school. He was late getting here. Now he takes off saying he's got to meet somebody else."

"So I take it you weren't napping but eavesdropping."

"That's why you're a detective, son." Marintha went into the kitchen and began wiping the table.

Bruce went into the den and flopped into an easy chair. He guessed he didn't know enough about his son's life, but what teenager wants a nosy parent prying into everything? Sure, Daniel had been in a little trouble at school, but it was nothing major. The deputies hauled in kids doing worse things every day. Daniel's shenanigans were just that, the actions of a hyperactive teenager with too much on his mind. He had given his son a good talking-to and threatened to take away the car if it happened again.

Now if only Bruce could find a way to get Marintha to quit harping on *him*.

SHERIFF MARTY McGARRITY'S OFFICE was an homage to his Scottish heritage. His family had deep roots in King's Grant, dating before the Revolutionary War, when the patriots took on the Tories for their scavenging ways among the struggling colonists. Bruce examined the certificates from heritage societies and reenactment groups as he waited for his boss to arrive. He was smiling at a photograph of the sheriff

76

posing proudly in the McGarrity family tartan when he real-ized Marty had sneaked up behind him.

"Something amusing there, Yeats?" Bruce turned to find McGarrity smiling as well. "My wife says most women's knees don't look that good in a skirt."

Bruce laughed. "You're a braver man than I am. You wouldn't ever catch me in a dress."

McGarrity drew himself into a salute. "Never ever tell a Scotsman he is wearing a dress," he said in a mock accent, failing miserably to hide his Southern drawl. He sat behind the desk and opened his copy of Bruce's report on the uniden-tified body.

"Making any progress, son?" he asked, flipping the pages so fast Bruce wondered how he could absorb any information.

"Afraid not. We've got nothing so far. Few clues to her identity—mainly physical stuff. I'm afraid this one's going to wind up in the cold case file."

McGarrity peered over the tops of his glasses. "That drifter discovered the body, what—a week ago? And already you're giving up? That's not like you at all, Bruce."

"I'm just saying what I see. There's nothing here to work with."

"You always have something to work with," McGarrity said, his voice stern. "Just because most of your cases have been quick solves up to now doesn't mean you give up on some-thing just because the answer isn't staring you right in the face. In case you've forgotten, you've got the other young woman as well. Have you given up on her, too?"

Bruce stared out the window, his view obscured by the vene-tian blinds that cut the sunlight into neat slices. He shrugged. "I can't work without leads."

The sheriff leaned back in his chair. "I have never known you to be this sloppy or quick to call a case closed," he said, watching Bruce. "I take it things haven't changed between you and Janelle."

Janelle. Bruce tried to avoid talking about her with any-one at the office. He didn't want anyone to think he couldn't handle his own problems. It had taken a long time to build his reputation as an investigator who wouldn't put up with any guff from anyone, suspects or witnesses. He certainly didn't want anyone to think he couldn't control his situation at home, that his wife would throw him out, or that his son would rebel against his authority.

Now he was at odds over it all. Janelle wouldn't tell him anything. And Daniel. He loved his son fiercely and tried to keep him off the path he had seen so many other young people take. Nevertheless, his strict discipline had been diluted with a streak of indulgence. Bruce couldn't help it. He wanted to give Daniel the things he hadn't had as a teenager. A car. The latest gizmos. His mother was right about one thing: The world had changed, and he had changed along with it.

"You going to answer me, or are you going to stare out that window all day?"

McGarrity's voice startled Bruce out of his musings. "Nothing's changed. Janelle and I can't talk without yelling. I'm surprised the neighbors haven't called the cops."

"You are the cops. They probably don't know what to think if you're shouting that loud." McGarrity reached into his desk and pulled out a brochure. "Maybe you ought to consider this."

Bruce picked up the slick pamphlet and looked it over. "You gotta be kidding," he said, sliding it back across the desk.

"The Christian Peace Officers is a good outlet for all the stress we have," the sheriff responded, pushing the brochure back. "We have a chaplain—Rev. Mercer. He specializes in the unique problems we face."

"What do y'all do, sit around praying for all these good-for-nothings we throw in the tank every day?"

"Sometimes," McGarrity replied, with a slight smile. "We meet, have a good meal, listen to a speaker. It's a good place to meet good people. People who believe in God."

"Well, I'd be about as comfortable as a jaybird in a pen full of cats."

McGarrity's eyebrows arched. "You don't believe in God?"

"You're not going to fire me, are you?"

"No. We don't discriminate based on religion here. You know that. I'm just trying to suggest that maybe you need an outlet for all this hostility you're building up."

"This ain't hostility. I'm just sick and tired of all the bull I have to put up with." Bruce rose, taking the file with him. He turned around and looked at the floor. "I appreciate the invitation, but it's just not my kind of thing. All that God stuff's for other people."

"What makes you think that?"

"He never listened to me. Or if he did, he never bothered answering."

"Did you ever stop to think that maybe you weren't listening back?" McGarrity replied, then shrugged. "The offer's open. As for the case, take another look. A good, long look. This girl belongs to somebody. Maybe not around here, but she used to walk and talk and breathe good fresh air. Even if she went bad, she deserves to be identified and buried somewhere besides a pauper's grave. Her killer and the person who tried to kill our other Jane Doe are still walking around free."

Bruce nodded and walked down the hall, where he shut his office door. He had hardly had time to sit and reopen the case file when a tiny knock interrupted his whirling thoughts. "Come in," he called out, irritated at the interruption.

The door nudged open. "Got a minute for a reporter desperate to fill her slot in the evening news?" Kelly slid inside and closed the door quickly behind her.

"What's wrong? The street guys aren't bringing in enough convenience store robbers to fill the time?" He went around and sat in the visitor's chair as Kelly leaned against the desk. "Is this what you've resorted to, hounding us desk jockeys?"

Kelly smiled. Bruce noticed that it wasn't her TV smile, the one that seemed forced and just a little too perky. He had noticed that this was a smile she seemed to reserve especially for him. "Are you ever serious?"

"All the time and way too much," he said. "So when are you going to take me up on my dinner invitation?"

Kelly sat in the chair next to him. "I'm still thinking it over."

"What's to think? I'm not living with my wife anymore. In fact, I think we might even be getting a divorce." He was surprised to hear himself saying the words. He hadn't even thought that far before. Now, for some reason, it just popped out.

Kelly blinked. "How does your son feel about that?"

Bruce wished he hadn't used the word. "Um, we haven't told him yet." How could you tell your son something you hadn't even discussed with your wife?

"I remember when my parents got divorced," Kelly said, her voice fading. "It was terrible. My sister and I thought we'd just die of all the crying we did."

Bruce went back to his chair. "I'm sorry you went through that. I didn't know."

"Divorce is really hard on kids, Bruce. Maybe you ought to think more about it. If you and your wife have any chance at all . . ."

"I don't need you giving me marital advice." Bruce flinched at his own harshness, and he could see the fear on Kelly's face. "I'm sorry. This case—"

"I know. It's okay. You're in a bad place right now."

You don't know the half of it, Bruce thought. "Speaking of the case, I really don't have anything new to tell you," he said, switching on the computer monitor and turning away so she couldn't see his expression. "I'm reexamining all the evidence. That's about it."

"Okay," Kelly said, rising and opening the door. "I am sorry about you and your wife. If you need to talk . . ."

"Yeah, Kelly. I'll let you know if there's anything new to report."

After she left, Bruce buried his head in his hands. Everything he had ever thought he knew about himself—his wife, his son, relationships, police work—was all coming apart like an old sofa left out in the weather. It had been so comfortable for so long. But now it was full of rips, faded from exposure to the harshness of wind and rain. Bruce wasn't the kind of man to go in for counseling. All that psychobabble. He had seen it get too many crooks out of trouble. Troubled childhoods, my foot, he usually said. Bruce had his own troubled childhood, but it hadn't turned him into Charles Manson or Ted Bundy.

And Christian Peace Officers? Bruce couldn't believe it. For one thing, he had never called himself a peace officer. With everything they saw every day—abuse, neglect, drug addiction, the crimes people committed to support their addictions, the shootings and stabbings—there was no way to keep peace among all that. He had heard so many preachers talk about how God *allowed* all this to happen, how he *allowed* people to die in horrendous ways. What kind of God *allows* people who love each other to fall out of love, making all that "til death do us part" garbage a lie?

Bruce turned his attention back to the case file. A skeleton with no identification, nothing to suggest who she was or where she was from. A woman left beaten senseless, locked inside her own body and mind. *Something else God allowed,* Bruce thought, studying the charts and reports, thinking haughtily that maybe this was one case where he had the upper hand over the man upstairs.

MARINTHA PULLED OPEN THE DRESSER DRAWER and dug underneath the antique lace linens until she found a faded shoebox, the lid tied on with a frayed lavender ribbon. She took it with her to the rocking chair that sat next to her bedroom window and placed it on her lap where she stared at it for a long time, afraid to open it. To her it was something special, yet it was also like that mythical story about Pandora's box. The memories it held were precious but deceptive. They masked a story she had vowed never to tell, a story she never wanted Bruce or Daniel to know.

As dusk fell, the light turned red through the low-lying clouds in the western sky, and she replaced the box in its hiding place, unopened, deciding the pleasure of how it all began wasn't worth the pain of how it all ended. She knew that sometimes you needed to box up the past and throw it away. Sometimes, though, that is the hardest thing anyone can ever do.

Ten

BRUCE SAT IN A HARD WOODEN CHAIR across from the principal's desk, feeling like he was the one being called on the carpet instead of his son. The setting brought on a sense of déjà vu, like it was only yesterday he had been the one in trouble, giving his own mother grief. He noticed Janelle was also shifting uncomfortably in her chair. Bruce imagined she was having similar thoughts. Neither of them would have won any gold stars for good behavior during their school days.

Mr. Hanks, the principal, came in, sat down behind the desk, and opened a file folder, which he studied for several moments before speaking, heightening the discomfort level.

"Your son is heading down a frightening path," Mr. Hanks said without preface. "His behavior is deteriorating daily, and I suggest you get him some help."

Bruce blinked and allowed himself a glance at Janelle. Her arms were folded tightly against her chest as if she were freezing cold. "I don't understand," she said without emotion. "I haven't had any trouble with him at home."

"From what I can gather, Mrs. Yeats, you're rarely there to know," the principal said, adjusting his glasses. "And neither are you." His gaze rested on Bruce.

"You have to understand—we're working to provide a future for Daniel. Money to attend college, a nice home . . ."

"A stable home is what he needs," the principal replied. "If he doesn't start getting his academic act together, there'll be no college either."

Bruce let out a breath. Mr. Hanks pulled no punches.

"What has Daniel done?" Janelle asked.

"He's created a number of disruptions in his classes."

Bruce leaned forward. "What kinds of disruptions?"

"Inciting pranks among his classmates. Making inappropriate remarks to teachers."

"Inappropriate how?"

"Profane, Mr. Yeats. We do not allow profanity here."

"Well, we don't allow it at home, either," Janelle said, a hard edge creeping into her voice.

"Which home?"

"He spends most of his time with his mother. Our schedules are crazy, but her job does allow her a more regular routine," Bruce offered.

"And does the law enforcement profession now encourage familial neglect?"

Bruce stood and leaned over the desk. "Now you listen here," he said, his voice rising as he shook Janelle's hand away from his arm. "We have never neglected our son. He's had everything a child needs."

"Really? Everything?" The principal leaned forward, his face inches away from Bruce's as if daring him to take the next step.

"What are you implying?" Janelle asked, watching Bruce.

"I'm saying your son is becoming emotionally stunted. He lacks direction, a sense of responsibility, focus."

"He has responsibilities. He helps out his grandmother after school. Janelle makes sure his homework is done."

Janelle looked down at her lap.

"Not according to his teachers," Mr. Hanks said, his tone softening. "Sit down, Mr. Yeats. I'm not accusing the two of you of anything. We seem to see this more and more. Kids who don't take anything seriously, who seem to think they have no future."

Bruce frowned. "None of this makes sense."

"Parenting is the world's most difficult profession. I doubt you would find anyone who would disagree with that. But when parents separate, when households are split, when discipline isn't consistent, when rules aren't consistent, that all has a devastating effect on the child. Children need limits, and Daniel is showing that he's willing to operate outside the boundaries of acceptable behavior."

The three sat silently until a bell rang somewhere in the building and the raucous sounds of teenagers changing classes filled the hallway outside.

"What kind of trouble is Daniel in?" Janelle asked quietly.

"He threw a desk across a classroom. That's a one-week suspension for a first offense." He took off his glasses and rubbed his eyes. "We're fortunate no one happened to be standing in its path or you'd be here arresting your own son. If it happens again, it may mean a longer suspension, a move to the alternative school, or even expulsion."

Bruce stood up and walked to the door. "We're going to straighten him out," he said, holding it open for Janelle. "You won't have any more problems with him."

"Famous last words, Mr. Yeats," said Mr. Hanks, closing the file and ringing his secretary to show in the next set of beleaguered parents.

In the parking lot, Janelle and Bruce stood between their cars, waiting for Daniel. Bruce checked his watch and folded his arms.

"Do you have a criminal to catch or something?" Janelle watched his face, looking for cracks in his composure.

"I have a meeting I need to get to."

High, thin clouds allowed only a slim glimpse of sunlight to fall across the chilly parking lot. Bruce thought of several things to say, then dismissed them all, not wanting to start another fight. Daniel emerged from the building and walked over to them.

"Daniel, this stops now," Bruce began, holding out his hand. "Give me your car keys."

Daniel glared at him before digging the keys from his pocket and slipping them in Bruce's palm. "You can hold the lectures, Dad." He tugged at the passenger door on Janelle's car, but it was locked. "Let me in, Mom."

"Your father has some things he wants to say to you."

"Father? Let's see now—is that a noun or a verb?"

Bruce grabbed his son's arm. "I see what Mr. Hanks was talking about now. Is this how he talks to you?" He looked at Janelle as Daniel wrested his arm away.

"Don't start that. I've done everything I know how to do with him," she said.

"Well, I guess it hasn't been enough."

Daniel turned and stomped across the pavement. "Don't walk away from me when I'm trying to talk to you," Bruce said, running after him.

"You were *trying* to talk to me? What a joke!"

Janelle appeared at his other arm. "Come on, let's go home. We're all too upset now. We'll talk about this later."

"Talk about it or yell about it?"

Bruce stuffed his hands in his pockets. "That's enough, son. Go with your mother."

Daniel sighed, took the keys his mother proffered, and went back to the car.

"We do need to talk about this," Janelle said to Bruce. "Sometime when you can be reasonable."

"I'm not being unreasonable."

"Stop it." She turned and got in the car, giving him one last cold look before driving away.

Bruce cranked the cruiser and drove to the sheriff's department, a complex of buildings that included courtrooms, offices, and the county jail. Sheriff McGarrity had already started the meeting when Bruce slipped into the back row.

". . . of the task force will include Riley Starks, Peter Wilson, and Bruce Yeats."

"What task force?" Bruce whispered to Peter, who sat next to him sipping a Mello Yello, trying not to rattle the wrapping on a pack of Nabs.

"Drug interdiction task force. Too many drugs getting past us on I-95 for the Scotsman's taste."

Bruce groaned. His desk was already piled ten inches deep with files needing paperwork updates. He was still trying to identify the body found in the woods and the woman in the nursing home. And now Daniel. He didn't know what to put first.

"Yeats, you want to give us an update on the Jane Doe cases?"

All eyes in the room turned to Bruce, unprepared for the sudden attention. Peter stuffed the crackers in his pocket.

"Nothing new to report," Bruce said, standing awkwardly and staring at the assembled deputies and clerical personnel. "Unless we get some leads, I don't see any progress in the foreseeable future."

McGarrity nodded. "Foreseeable future, huh." He looked back down at his clipboard. "I tell you—all of you—if we don't see some results, some reductions in robberies, some clues dug up in some of these unsolved larcenies and assaults, our foreseeable future is going to be filled with some bad press and some upset citizenry. And frankly I don't blame them."

"We're doing the best we can," Riley Starks replied from the other side of the room.

"Your best isn't good enough. Our solve rate is below the state average."

"We don't have enough people to handle all the cases," Bruce said defensively.

"I know that. The budget's tight, at least until next year. Maybe then we can add some new hires. But right now we've got a crime wave, and I'm depending on all of you to prioritize and make the best of an uncomfortable situation." He picked up the clipboard and left the room abruptly, leaving the assembly grumbling so loudly it sounded like a Harley Davidson motorcycle convention. "Bruce, my office."

Bruce followed McGarrity out, feeling as if he were returning to Mr. Hanks's office for a new round of reproach.

"How's your boy?" he asked, motioning Bruce to sit down.

"How'd you know?"

"Don't you know by now I know everything there is to know about everybody here?" A thin smile crossed McGarrity's face.

"He's had a little trouble. Nothing I can't handle."

McGarrity nodded. "I know I'm adding lots of pressure here, putting you on the task force."

"It was nice of you to let me know first." Bruce couldn't keep the sarcasm from his voice.

"You're the best investigator on the force, and you have the most experience with this sort of thing. The other officers can learn from how you handle yourself here. I wouldn't have assigned you if I didn't think you could handle it," said the sheriff. "If you can't—"

"I can handle it." Bruce stood to leave. "Was there anything else?"

"No. Just look out for your boy. Being a cop's son ain't an easy life."

Neither is being a teenager's father, Bruce thought.

Back in his office, he found several messages on his voice mail. "Bruce, I thought about your offer for dinner, and if it still holds, I'd like to see you." Kelly Karlisle's voice lifted his spirits. "Call me, and we'll set a time."

Task force, shmask force. Bruce deserves a little night on the town first, he thought, picking up the phone and dialing what was definitely the wrong number.

IT SEEMED AS IF EVERY POT, pan, bowl, and utensil in Marintha's kitchen was dirty, and the room felt as hot as a July afternoon before a thunderstorm. She and Etta had spent the past two days preparing for the Manna Methodist Church's annual November bake sale and flea market. At one point, Etta pointed out that it might have been easier for them to go out and gather fleas than to bake so many different items.

All available surfaces—those not covered by dirty dishes—were overlaid with pecan pies, pound cakes, chocolate brownies, and peanut butter cookies, packed into plastic bags or covered with brightly colored plastic wrap. The two women had begun before daylight, stopping only once to eat pimiento cheese sandwiches and to sample some of the brownies, being careful not to eat up the merchandise in spite of the tempting aromas that permeated the house. After a while, they had their duties down to a science. While one measured and mixed, the other filled pans and tended the stove and wall oven.

At 5:00 P.M., exhausted, Marintha and Etta agreed they were ready for a full-time bakery job down at the Piggly Wiggly. They now sat in the living room with their unshod feet propped on soft ottomans, sipping iced tea in spite of the fact that the temperature outside had dropped nearly to freezing.

"That is the best thing I have ever tasted," Etta exclaimed, fishing out the lemon and placing it on a napkin.

"Amen," said Marintha, wiggling her toes. Every joint in her body ached. She knew Etta's had to hurt, too, though her friend would sooner die with her lips sewn shut than admit she needed an aspirin.

Lamplight cast a warm glow between them. Marintha and Etta had been friends for more than thirty years, and silence came to them like a chenille pillow, soft and comfortable, the way it does for old friends. Marintha often thanked God that he had sent her such a wonderful Christian companion. Even before Etta's husband had died, a hard death from cancer, they had been nearly inseparable and talked on the phone daily, each interested in all the details of the other's life, no matter how mundane or trivial. And although Etta was black and Marintha was white, they had never experienced prejudice against their friendship. Marintha felt truly blessed.

Suddenly Etta groaned.

"Aha!" Marintha shouted. "I knew sooner or later you'd admit your feet hurt."

"I ain't groaning about my feet, girl! I was just thinking that now we got to get up and clean that messy kitchen, then we got to carry all that food over to the church reception hall."

At that, Marintha let out a groan as well. She looked at the old clock ticking away on the mantel, marking off the seconds and minutes and hours in the same plodding way it had for the last century, when it had been her grandmother's prized possession, a wedding gift from Marintha's grandfather.

"We've got a while," Marintha said, settling back and closing her eyes for a second. "Maybe Bruce will be home soon and he can help us."

Etta shot her a withering look. "You know that's the first time you've mentioned your son all day?"

Marintha opened her eyes. "I didn't feel like talking about him and Janelle."

"Well, if you don't talk to me, who you going to talk to about Bruce and Janelle? Besides the Lord, that is."

"There's not much to tell. He and Janelle are still separated. I see Daniel from time to time when he comes to work on the yard, though he hardly takes the time to speak with me. Nothing I haven't already told you." She sighed. "I guess when you get to a certain point, you're just not that interesting to your children or your grandchildren anymore."

Etta laughed. "Since when were we ever interesting to our children? Seems like they always want us to be interested in them until they get to be teenagers, then they forget we're alive, and we turn out to be the stupidest people on the face of the earth until they hit middle age when they find out that, I'll be, Mama's the wisest woman on the face of the earth!"

"Truer words were never spoken," Marintha said, joining her friend in laughter, although she wondered just how long it would take Bruce to make that discovery. Car lights swept across the window, and she leaned forward to see Bruce pulling in. "I can't believe it."

"Believe what?" Etta asked, peering into the driveway.

"Bruce is actually coming home on time for once." She struggled to her feet and plodded to the kitchen barefooted, Etta following behind. Bruce came in the back door and surveyed the wreckage.

"Did Willy Wonka's Chocolate Factory explode in here?" he asked, warily examining the piled-up dishes before trying to sneak a brownie from its cooling rack.

"Those are for the church bake sale," Marintha scolded, allowing him to take the brownie anyway. "We need you to help us carry everything over to the church. They're setting up tonight."

"I don't have time, Mama," he said, finishing the chocolate square and washing his hands in the small gap between the spigot and a precarious stack of mixing bowls.

"But you're home early. You got an urgent TV show to watch?"

Bruce shook his head. "Got a date."

Marintha and Etta exchanged wide-eyed looks before Etta busied herself at the sink, her back to the others. Marintha crooked her finger at Bruce. They went into the living room, where she closed the door.

"What are you thinking? Obviously you're not thinking, or you wouldn't have said what I just think you said."

"What's the big deal, Mama? Janelle and I are separated. We're probably going to get divorced. . . ."

"Probably ain't so," Marintha said, trying to keep the anger out of her voice and failing. "Just because you *might* doesn't mean you *will.*"

"Me and Janelle haven't got a prayer."

"Maybe if you said one you might," said Marintha, folding her arms. "You and Janelle have been together since you were teenagers. I remember when you first fell in love. Two people were never more suited to each other."

"Well, we may have been suited then, but we're not now," Bruce replied, sitting on the couch and propping his arms across his knees.

"I don't care if you are separated. It's adultery to get involved with another woman when you're still married."

Bruce looked down at his feet, feeling the force of his mother's words, trying to fashion a reply. "I have a right to get on with my life. And if I want to go out and have a little fun, then there's nothing you can do about it."

"There might be nothing I can do, but there sure is a lot I can say," Marintha countered defiantly. "It's not time for you to get on with your life yet, because you still have a lot of unfinished business. Think about the example you'd be setting for your son."

"That his dad's not the kind to stay fixated on the past? Boy, you're somebody to be talking to *me* about living in the past, Mama. You've been living there my whole life, and I don't intend to set that same example for my son."

Marintha turned away so her son couldn't see the tears that burned her eyes. "I held myself together and created a good life for you after your father left us," she said quietly. "I always tried to set a Christian example for you. I'm only sorry it didn't take." She put on her shoes and went into the kitchen where she proceeded to load the baked goods into boxes. *Maybe my works will do somebody some good,* she prayed silently as Etta continued to wash the dishes. *I just don't know what I'm going to do with my son. I guess I'll have to leave him up to you.*

BRUCE STOOD IN THE RESTAURANT BAR, looking at his watch and wondering if Kelly had forgotten the time. The evening news would have ended by now, and she'd be off work.

He flexed his hands, realizing he had been clenching his fists. His mother's words had stuck hard in his mind, and the more he tried pushing them away, the more prominently they dominated his thoughts. Maybe he wasn't always there for Daniel in terms of time, but he believed he was always there in the ways that counted. If only he could say that about his own father.

He still remembered the day he came home from school and found his mother crying at the kitchen table. She sat there, her shoulders shaking, as he tried to find out what the problem was. He became frightened and thought about calling 9-1-1. Marintha had never cried that way before, at least not that Bruce had seen. Sure, she had shed tears when first her father, then her mother died, but not like this. Worse than if somebody died.

When she finally raised her head and realized he was there, now crying himself, she quickly dried her eyes and gathered him to her. "It's just us now, Brucie," she had whispered, covering his head with kisses. "Daddy's gone, and it's just us."

Bruce hadn't understood what she meant, thinking that his father had died. It had taken a long time to realize that the man had simply left them—packed his clothes and walked away without so much as a backward glance or a phone call to ever see how he was.

He thought his father would be proud of the man he had grown to be—not that he would ever care. If he had cared, he would have come looking for Bruce, come to see him long ago. But on the birthdays and Christmases and Easters that passed through the years, Bruce's father never came. So Bruce's bitterness grew.

It must have been his mother's fault. She had to have done something to drive him away. He believed that in his heart, but he had never said the words, keeping his resentment locked inside. Bruce had looked at his own actions again and again and decided he had done nothing that could have made his own father abandon him. For years he watched Marintha, wondering what she had done to make his father leave.

Tonight he had come all around asking her, but he had reined himself in. He was living under his mother's roof, after all, and right now he couldn't afford to alienate her. She was right about one thing: After his father left, she had provided a good home for him. And they had had a lot of good times. But somehow that didn't take away all the hurt. A tap on Bruce's shoulder startled him from his thoughts.

"Are you Bruce Yeats?" A waiter holding a cordless phone stood beside him. Bruce nodded. "You have a call."

"Yeats here," he said gruffly into the phone.

"You don't have to sound so mad about it." A soft female laugh emanated through the line.

"I'm sorry, Kelly. I thought it was probably the office. I left my pager at home."

"It's okay. I called to say I can't make it. I have to cover a city council meeting."

Bruce sighed. "You didn't know about this before? I had reservations."

"I'm sorry. The reporter who regularly covers the meetings called in sick. I don't have a choice."

"Okay. Well, I guess we'll have to see each other another time."

"I'll call you."

"I'll be waiting."

Bruce handed the phone back over the bar and left the restaurant. Getting in his car, he noticed he felt less tense. It had been a long time since he had been on a date. Maybe he wasn't as ready as he thought.

eleven

BLINDED BY THE GLARE from all the TV lights, Bruce was tempted to put on his sunglasses but decided that might be a little much for the month of December, a little too Hollywood. This was only local television, after all, so he decided to go with the squinty-eyed look.

The state crime lab hadn't completed its facial reconstruction from the unidentified skull; meanwhile, he had decided to appeal to the media for help. An exhaustive review of all the evidence obtained at the scene revealed nothing new that would help them identify this victim. His follow-up interviews with Jonesy Jones had not given him any additional information—the vagrant either couldn't or wouldn't provide any useable details about the man who dumped the body.

Chances were that even this effort would do little to advance the case. Sheriff McGarrity was on Bruce's back almost daily to solve it. In spite of all the time he was forced to devote to the drug task force, Bruce had spent hours sifting through missing person reports, reading forensics journals, searching for some way to identify these women.

It would help if someone were looking for them, Bruce often thought. But that didn't seem to be the case. It was as if neither woman had a past—no family, no friends, no one to care if they were alive or dead.

In domestic violence cases, shouting a wish that the other were dead was common for one party or the other, at least until the responding officer slapped on the cuffs. Then a sudden round of remorse, apology, forgiveness, and begging the officers to let the offender go generally followed. He had seen love—a sick kind of love—transcend violence.

This he couldn't fathom. These women were missing from somewhere. It was like that old saying about how nature abhors a vacuum. It was like they had vanished from wherever they had come from and the space had simply filled, and life had gone on as if they never existed.

Bruce didn't know what he would do if something like that happened to Daniel or Janelle. Although their relationship had deteriorated to the point of bare existence, he knew that if one of them disappeared, the sole purpose of his life would become finding out what had happened.

He squinted at the lights and read from his prepared statement.

"On November 4, the decomposed remains of a woman were found in a wooded area in the southern end of King's Grant County. Extensive efforts to identify these remains have failed. All we know is that she was most probably a white female between the ages of eighteen and thirty. Dental records do not match any known missing persons from the state of South Carolina.

"We are asking anyone who knows anything about this woman to contact us here at the sheriff's department or to use our Crime Stopper's number if you wish to remain anonymous."

"Do you know the cause of death?" Kelly stood to one side, pen and pad at the ready, wearing her reporter's face.

"We believe she was the victim of massive trauma to the body. Portions of the skeleton suggest evidence of stab wounds and a severe beating. The medical examiner discovered several fractures during the autopsy. The medical examiner says it's possible she could have died of massive internal bleeding caused by these injuries." He pointed to another reporter.

"Is there a reward for information?"

"We have a small Crime Stopper's reward for information leading to the arrest and conviction of whoever committed this murder." *If her family was looking, we might have a bigger one.*

"So it is confirmed as a homicide?"

"Yes. Based on some information we received from an eyewitness, a white male may have killed her, approximately six feet tall, age and race undetermined, dressed in blue jeans and a hooded sweatshirt."

"Who is your eyewitness?"

"I can't reveal that information at this time."

"Do you believe this murder is related to the attempted murder of the other Jane Doe?"

Bruce took a deep breath before responding. "We are reexamining that case as well, but right now we have no specific information that links the two crimes. We are treating these as separate cases."

He held up his hands to stop the questions. "What we need now is the public's help. If we can find out the identities of either of these women, then maybe we can determine what happened to them. Thank you."

Bruce turned and went back into the law enforcement center to find a man waiting for him at his office door.

"Can I help you?" Bruce asked, sure he had not seen him there before.

"This is for you." He handed Bruce an envelope and walked away quickly.

"Wait!" he called, but the man had rounded the corner and was gone.

Bruce stared at the envelope for a moment before opening it. He was not prepared for what he found inside, although he couldn't really say that he hadn't been expecting it.

PETITION FOR DIVORCE the paper stated in bold capital letters across the top. He lay the document on his desk without reading it and looked up to find Marty standing in the doorway.

"Who's suing you? Please tell me it's not against the department."

Bruce smiled ruefully. "Nope. Just my wife suing to get out of our marriage."

"That's what you've been wanting, isn't it?" The sheriff settled into the chair across the desk from Bruce. "Cut the ties, live your own life."

"It's one thing to think about it; it's another thing to see it spelled out in black and white," Bruce replied.

"Have you and Janelle tried counseling?"

"You're kidding me," Bruce huffed, placing the papers in his desk drawer before slamming it louder than he meant to. "Sitting around talking about our troubles with some stranger who wouldn't know real life if it bit him in the face?"

"It's not so bad."

"You're not telling me . . ."

"About ten years ago." McGarrity rubbed his face. "This job takes its toll on everyone, Bruce. Including the man in charge. Unless you put it in the hands of the one who is really in charge."

"You're not going to go quoting that God stuff at me again, are you? I already told you, he doesn't want anything to do with me."

"He's always got something to do with you, Bruce, but you have to let him."

Bruce leaned back in his chair. "I don't know if there's any hope for me and Janelle. Too much has happened."

"If you ask me, it hasn't been that much."

"How would you know?" Bruce felt his skin grow hot. He hadn't confided in McGarrity recently, just given him the spare details of the separation.

"I used to be an investigator, too, you know. I like to know what's going on with the people who work for me." He allowed himself a small smile. "I saw Janelle at a restaurant a couple of weeks ago."

"You talked to my wife behind my back?" Bruce fought to control the sudden tremor in his voice. "You talked about my marriage with my wife and not me?"

97

"Somebody had to talk to somebody. I sure couldn't get any straight answers out of you."

Bruce let out a breath. "So what did she tell you? I beat her up, I cheated, I went on drunken rampages?"

"No," McGarrity said quietly. "She said you fell out of love with her."

All the anger drained from Bruce's body, replaced with a heavy sadness that threatened to crush his chest. He found himself unable to speak. When he did, his voice came out as a whisper. "She said I didn't love her anymore?"

"Yes. She seems to think you love all this," he gestured around the room, "more than you could ever love her."

"That is not true. That is simply not true. It's the other way around. Janelle doesn't love me or she would not be serving me divorce papers. She's known for years that my job isn't your typical nine-to-five. She knew the sacrifices she'd have to make."

"But what sacrifices did you make? Or did you both refuse to make any?"

Bruce had no reply.

McGarrity rose and leaned across the desk. "You have to open your heart, Bruce. Quit trying to bring the tough guy routine home. Leave the job here, son."

"That's easy to say."

The sheriff nodded. "You know, we got a whole bunch of guys here who've been through similar circumstances."

"You're talking about those Christian cops."

"Those Christian cops are human beings, just like you, Bruce. You ought to at least come and hear us out."

Bruce looked absently at the piles of paperwork covering his desk. "I'll think about it."

"Don't just think. Do."

"What, are you Yoda now?" Bruce allowed himself a smile.

"Nope, just a wise and wary Scotsman," McGarrity replied in his fake accent as he left Bruce's office. Bruce got up to close the door, only for Kelly to materialize in front of him.

This is not a good time. "Hey, Kel. Listen, if you need anything else for your story . . ."

"I'm not here about the story. I just wanted to know if my rain check on our dinner is still good." She looked up at him, smiling, her head tilted to one side.

Bruce thought about his mother's words, then tried to shunt the thought aside. It refused to go. "I'm really busy right now. McGarrity's on my case, my kid's having fits, my wife—" He stopped himself and turned away.

"What about your wife?" Kelly followed him, her arms folded now.

"It's nothing for you to be concerned about."

She nodded. "So then you're just too busy."

"That's all, just busy. Maybe in a few days we can get together. When I get some of my casework cleaned up." He looked at Kelly's face, but her expression was blank.

"I know the runaround when I hear it."

"It's not a runaround, Kel; I just don't have the time." He didn't try to squelch his anger.

"Fine," Kelly said. "You call me. I won't call you."

She left before Bruce could react. He fell back in his chair, retrieved the papers from his desk drawer, and studied the legal jargon for a few minutes before throwing them down.

He had never meant for it to come to this. When he and Janelle separated, he thought it would do them both good to have some time away from each other, kind of like a forced vacation. Put a little fresh air between them. Then they could come back together, go on with their lives.

It had not taken him long to figure out that separation doesn't work that way. If their marriage had cracks before, it was certainly broken now. He couldn't figure out how to go back, either.

Every time he saw Janelle, he felt as if she was ripping his heart a little more, the way his mother used to tear strips of fabric to make bandages for overseas missionaries when he was a kid. Every word between them became a ravel, something else to be ripped off and thrown away.

Time was he thought he could never live without her, could never find another woman like her, one who understood his mind and his drive, the way the job made him feel. Maybe that was the problem. All the time he had been expecting her to understand his choice, he had never taken the time to understand hers.

Nursing wasn't an easy job, either. Stressful, unpredictable, time-consuming. Like Bruce, Janelle had gone into the medical profession to help people, only to find that it hurt her in ways she hadn't considered. Losing patients—when it was a gunshot victim, it was the same as it was for Bruce. Something neither one of them could stop, no matter whether they wielded a gun or a hypodermic needle.

Bruce looked across the desk and noticed a piece of paper lying in the chair where McGarrity had sat. It was a brochure for the Christian Peace Officers. He picked it up and read it before placing it on top of the divorce papers. Then he picked up the phone. Bruce suddenly remembered that he needed to call his wife.

Twelve

RINGS OF CONDENSATION SPLOTCHED the polished bar surface. Wanda traced one with her index finger, turning it into a puddle as she stared into her glass.

Few people hung around this late at night. Night owls and barflies. The usual suspects when it came to drowning your sorrows and a few other clichés she could think of.

When she looked into the glass, she saw Kendall, and Derek, and everyone who had ever hurt her—everyone she had hurt in return. She held the glass close to her face, watching mirages float among the melting ice, inhaling the aroma like it was fine wine instead of cheap bar-brand booze.

Wanda had sat like that for nearly an hour, picking up the glass and putting it down. Her thoughts darted from one memory to another, never settling on one, tearing away from the good ones to concentrate on the bad.

The drink was the only one she had ordered. She had yet to drink a drop.

Mel and Lottie came to mind. Their friendship had made her sobriety bearable.

Kendall walked by, cursing Wanda's existence and her absence of motherly virtue.

Derek walked out, leaving her in a drunken heap on the floor, begging him to stay. *I'll get sober*, she had cried. *I can be a good wife. I swear I can.* Kendall had clung to his leg, begging him to take her along. *I'll come back for you someday, honey,* he had promised Kendall. *When I get settled, I'll come get you, and we'll live far away from Mommy.*

Another broken promise to their daughter.

Until now.

Kendall wasn't coming to see her, the mother who had been there, though she couldn't remember most of it. She was going to see her deadbeat dad, the man who walked out without a backward toss of a child support check or even a belated birthday card. His leaving had left Wanda and Kendall in the street, with nowhere to go and no means to get there.

I am with you always, Wanda.

What was that voice? She looked at the drink again. Maybe it was all the cigarette smoke making her dizzy. She wasn't used to it anymore.

I will never leave you nor forsake you.

She looked around, but no one was there. Only the bartender drying glasses at the other end of the bar. The voice kept speaking. Tears welled in her eyes.

I died for you, Wanda, and I have washed away your sins.

Wanda pulled some dollar bills from her purse and threw them on the counter. She stumbled out to the street, dazed despite not drinking, and somehow managed to walk home, although once she arrived she couldn't remember getting there. She found the door standing wide open, just as she had left it. She went inside, closed it, and locked it.

The boxes weren't stacked as high now. She could see over them, see the solitary life to which she had come. A life alone, without family, without the ones she loved most, loved even when she didn't realize it, didn't realize her own need for their love in return. Lost—it was the only word she could use to describe herself. Lost in time, within her own family, within her life, the fragile sobriety she had finally claimed.

The best position to look up from is down.

The minister's words from last Sunday's sermon echoed in her mind.

In her bedroom, she fell to her knees.

"Lord," she cried, her face pressed against the comforter, "I'm so weak. I nearly gave in tonight. I don't know why you came to me then, but I'm glad you did. I need you to help me keep my eyes on what's important. I forgot that for a while.

"I have to find my girl and see if she'll forgive me for all I've done to her. I don't know if Derek will. I don't know if Kendall can. I'm asking you for this one thing, and I hope you can see your way to letting me have it, even though I don't deserve it. I'm praying this in the name of your Son, Jesus. Amen."

Wanda got up, spent and weary, and went into the kitchen where she picked up the pile of journals and stacked them neatly on the table, taking out the one she had been reading before she went to the bar. She found the page that mentioned Derek and forced herself to continue reading.

I wish I could see Mama again, but I don't know if I can without a lot of memories and baggage getting dredged up. I know I need to forgive her and I've tried. I've tried to understand why she is the way she is, and I'm trying not to hold her mistakes against her.

Sometimes I wish life could be like it was a long, long time ago. Me and Mama and Daddy all together on the beach (without Mama's cooler, of course), and we would laugh and talk and play. We could be a family again. Together. I think that's what I miss most of all. That we haven't been together. That they haven't been together, when I know he really loved her.

She read on for several more pages, at times laughing when Kendall remembered a good time, crying when she recounted the bad and what it took for her to withstand her own memories. When she finished, she resolved to call Derek in the morning.

Maybe once in their life they could do something together. Maybe together they could find their daughter.

THE PHONE RANG for what seemed like an eternity, and Wanda nearly hung up when a gruff voice answered.

"Yeah."

Still Derek. He never minced words when he could slice them neatly.

"Is this Derek Hunter?"

The man was silent for a moment. "Wanda?"

"I'm surprised you remember my voice after all these years."

"I would never forget your voice."

The softness she heard surprised her. Her anger from the night before had long melted away, and she found herself searching for what she wanted to say, although she had been up half the night rehearsing it.

"You still there?"

"Yeah, I'm here."

"Was there some reason you called?"

She cleared her throat. "Derek, have you heard from Kendall?"

"I talked with her a couple times a while back. We talked about maybe getting together. Have you seen her?"

"No. That's why I'm calling." She took a deep breath. "Kendall's missing."

"Missing? What do you mean 'missing'?"

"I mean I went to see her. She's not there, and no one knows where she is or what happened to her." Wanda hated doing this over the phone, wishing she could see Derek's face and gauge his reaction.

"I thought that maybe she had just changed her mind."

"About going to see you?"

"How did you . . ."

"I read her journals."

Wanda took several minutes filling him in on her attempts to find their daughter, keeping her eye on the clock, not wanting to be late for work.

"Last night I read in her journal that she was planning to visit you, so I decided I should call."

Derek cleared his throat. "We never had any definite date. She just said maybe she would drive up one weekend. I'm always home, so I told her when she got ready, just come on. When I didn't hear anything else from her, I figured maybe she had thought better of it. I didn't call her back, because I assumed she'd decided she really didn't want me in her life."

Wanda ran her palm over the stack of journals. "I felt the same way. I just don't know what to do now."

"From what you've described, I don't think we have a choice but to look for her."

We. Twenty years melted away with that one word. "I don't see how, Derek. You're up in Virginia. My car's in the shop...."

"The Lord always provides a way," he said quietly. He was silent for so long that Wanda thought they had lost the connection. "I left my family. I loved all of you, Wanda, but I didn't know what to do. I should've helped you more instead of leaving you like a coward." He let out a deep breath. "I'm so sorry for what I did to you."

"That cuts both ways. I drove you away. I only thought about myself, my own pain, and I blamed you for things that weren't your fault. Since I've been sober, I've tried to make amends to everyone, and I thought maybe Kendall would give me another chance." Her voice broke. "Now I don't think I'm going to get that chance."

"Did you ever think that you and I would ever speak again?"

"Not really. I guess I thought there'd never be a reason to."

"But here we are, talking like all those years and miles aren't standing between us." She heard papers shuffling in the background. "I'm coming down there."

"You can't just up and leave your job."

"Yeah, I can," he said. "I own the company, so that ought to be good for some time off. I'm coming down there, and I don't want any argument. Our gal's missing, and we have to find her. This is too big for you to try to do alone."

"I'm not alone. I have friends to help."

"But they're not family."

"What about your—your wife?"

He laughed. "Didn't you know? I screwed up another marriage after ours. I've been divorced for years."

"You never had any more children?"

"Would have liked to, but I made such a mess the first time around, I didn't think that risking it again was fair."

"We sure have made a mess of things, Derek."

"Yeah, but now at least we got the chance to make it all right. And the place to start is with Kendall."

They spoke for a few more minutes, ending with Derek promising to let her know when he got into town. She hung up and sat staring at the wall.

THE FIRST TIME SHE SAW HIM was at a high school dance. He was wearing a white tuxedo with a red boutonniere; she was dressed in white as well. Their friends pushed them together on the dance floor, and his crystal blue eyes and the way his hands met across the back of her waist entranced her.

Even then she was drinking, not much, just a little to feel high, light, friendly. Derek hadn't even noticed. It just seemed that all they did that night was gaze into each other's eyes, imagining what it would be like to stay that way forever, young and close, looking forward to life's adventures that had been put there especially for the two of them.

Wanda shook her head and looked at the clock. Late for work.

She grabbed her purse and dashed out the door. Running for the bus stop, she repeated Kendall's name over and over to herself. *She's all I have to live for now. She's my only reason to be.*

Derek had changed. Wanda studied his face as they returned to her apartment in his rental car. She had taken the bus to meet him at the airport, where he had insisted on renting the sedan for their mutual use until she got her car fixed. Generosity hadn't been one of his virtues, but he seemed to have developed many that were revealed moment by moment.

"You're awfully quiet," he said, driving confidently through rush hour traffic.

"I'm just noticing the changes," she said, feeling as if she were squeezing her voice through a straw. Wanda hadn't felt so shy in years.

"Are they good or bad?"

"Good," she replied, smiling. "I'm just having trouble believing that you're really here."

"In the flesh. With a lot more of it than I used to have."

They broke into laughter. Wanda could say the same thing for herself.

Wanda checked her laughter. Her daughter—their daughter—was missing, and here they were cutting up like teenagers. Derek seemed to read her mind, and his expression turned serious as well. They drove along, quiet except for Wanda's directions until they reached her apartment. Derek already had reservations at a motel, but she wanted to show him Kendall's belongings and her journals before he checked in.

The stacks of boxes in her living room had dwindled as she unpacked them and stored the items carefully in her closet and the guest bedroom—a room she had begun to think of as Kendall's room. A place Kendall could stay when, and if, they found her alive, in whatever condition that might be. She wouldn't permit herself to think of the alternative.

"You look like you're doing pretty good for yourself here," Derek said, making himself comfortable on the sofa as Wanda fixed glasses of tea and brought the journals over to the coffee table.

"I'm doing better than I've done in years. Once I stopped drinking, it seems like my life finally started falling into place." She smiled. "In some ways, anyway."

Derek stirred his tea with his index finger, mixing in the lemon. It was a gesture Wanda had forgotten. He wiped his hand on a napkin and picked up the first journal.

"The early ones are hardest to read," she said, watching him flip through the pages, reading at random. If he had any emotional response, it didn't show on his face.

Wanda busied herself in the kitchen, tidying up places that didn't need tidying as Derek pored over the notebooks. Finally

107

she returned and found him reading the last journal. He snapped it shut and looked at her. "So, what's the plan?" Again, to the point.

She outlined her scheme for traveling the likely route Kendall would have taken. "I would have left by now if my car hadn't died on me."

"Where's your maps?"

"Over here." He joined her at the dining room table, where she spread out the papers, roads and highways outlined with red and blue markers, with circles marking the major interchanges.

"There's so many places she could have gotten off the interstate, Wanda. It's like looking for a flea on a black cat. Too many jumping off points."

Wanda sighed. "I don't know what else to do. The police won't take me seriously, and I don't have the money to hire a detective."

Derek pulled out a chair. "I'm going with you."

"What?" Wanda couldn't believe what he was saying.

"I said, I'm coming with you. You can't do this alone. If something happened to Kendall out there traveling alone, then something could happen to you, and she's going to need you when we find her."

With. We. They were words Wanda hadn't heard in years, only recently from Lottie, Mel, and Mandy, but somehow not in the same way. Derek was staring at her, waiting for a reply, but she couldn't find her voice.

"Unless you don't want me to . . ."

"I need all the help I can get," she said finally, her resolve returning.

"So when do you want to leave?"

Wanda hesitated, staring at him, wondering how he could be so trusting of her after all she had done. "Are you sure about this? It's been so many years . . ."

He took her hand. "You know, I see in you the woman you were meant to become, the woman I hoped you would become. Someone who cares about somebody besides herself." He kissed her forehead. "I may have left you, Wanda, but I never forgot you. I never forgot that girl I fell in love with."

As he turned to leave, Wanda touched his arm. "I don't know how to thank you for doing this."

"We have to find Kendall. She's my daughter, and I didn't do right by her either. This is something we have to do together." He left, promising to call her later that night to firm up plans for their journey.

Wanda took the photograph of Kendall from her purse and traced the outline of her daughter's face. "Daddy's back," she said, her eyes filling. "He's here to help bring you home."

As THEY SPED AROUND THE INTERSTATE on-ramp the next morning, Wanda fought to control her feelings. At last, she was going to find her daughter, her ex-husband at her side. She and Derek had hardly had time to get reacquainted, and now here they were taking this trip together. They agreed before leaving that they would rent separate motel rooms, split the gas and meal expenses, and spend a maximum of two weeks on their quest. If they hadn't found anything by then, they would return home and regroup.

Her hands shook as she unfolded the map. Derek must have noticed from the corner of his eye, because he reached over and took her left hand in his right one. "We are going to find her," he said. The confidence in his voice overwhelmed her.

"I wish I could be as sure as you are."

"I feel it. I just wish I had called you sooner or done something myself. Called Kendall back. Something." He let go of her hand and concentrated on the road. Wanda bent to the map, pinpointing their first exit and consulting her legal pad for the location of the first sheriff's department.

A stack of flyers that Mandy had created on the office computer lay on the backseat, the word MISSING in tall, bold letters across the top of each one. They planned to plaster the flyers at every gas station and convenience store along the way. "Saturation coverage," as Derek had described it.

The size of the task they had undertaken was just dawning on Wanda. She loved Kendall and would give her own life if that of her daughter could continue. Now that they were on the road, her plan seemed crazy, even to her. If only she could turn back the clock, live her life over, avoid the mistakes, live her life the way the Lord intended. But she couldn't go back.

Blacktop receded beneath the wheels, and time raced forward. They hurtled into the future, looking for their daughter, for a way to redeem their pasts. They traveled now on hope and faith, searching for clues, trying to find their own way, their daughter's way, the way back to each other.

"You're deep in thought over there," Derek said, looking in the rearview mirror.

"Just thinking about regrets."

"Like the old Sinatra song."

"What?"

"Sinatra. 'I did it my way.'" One thing hadn't changed. Derek's inability to carry a tune. Wanda found herself smiling.

"We did it our way, all right. The wrong way."

"Yeah, Wanda, but now we're going to make it right." There was that confidence again.

Wanda pointed to the green sign overhead. "Our first exit's coming up."

"Are you ready?" Derek merged with the exiting traffic.

"No," Wanda replied. "If I waited until I was ready, I'd never have accomplished anything." *Just let me accomplish this one thing, Lord. Let us find our daughter. Maybe then we can think about the next thing.* She glanced at Derek. *Whatever that might be.*

Thirteen

MACHINES TICKED OFF THE MOMENTS of the young woman's life with muted beeps and blips. Marintha came here every couple of weeks and sat with her, talking to her, treating her like a mother should treat a daughter. She brushed the girl's dark hair, which the nurses had cut short. The long, straight locks had been so matted with blood when she was admitted, it had been easier that way.

She had been found the day Bruce and Janelle had separated. Marintha would never forget the darkness, not only of the sky that threatened summer storms, but of the feelings that filled her heart, the sorrow for her son, her daughter-in-law, her grandson. Then the call had come in. A woman found, viciously beaten, close to death.

She had followed Bruce to the hospital, hoping she could bring some comfort to the girl's family when they were found. Yet as the night wore on, and the sun rose the next morning, hopes began to fade that the authorities would find her family. In fact, they never found anything, unlike the second Jane Doe, whose pearl pendant was now saved in an evidence bag in the police lockup. She had never told Etta about the necklace, because she knew it was evidence, although she secretly wished Bruce would release the information. Someone might recognize it and in turn know to whom it belonged and come forward with the information.

Opening her Bible to 1 Corinthians, chapter 13, she began to read aloud: "If I speak in the tongues of men and of angels, but have not love, I am only a resounding gong or a clanging cymbal. If I have the gift of prophecy and can fathom all mysteries and all knowledge, and if I have a faith that can move mountains, but have not love, I am nothing. If I give all I possess to the poor and surrender my body to the flames, but have not love, I gain nothing.

"Love is patient, love is kind. It does not envy, it does not boast, it is not proud. It is not rude, it is not self-seeking, it is not easily angered, it keeps no record of wrongs."

She repeated these last words to herself. *Love keeps no record of wrongs.* The letters that lay buried in the dresser drawer. Did that count as a record? Did the fact that she took them out from time to time and lived the hurt all over again—did that count as keeping track of the wrongs done to her and Bruce? Marintha always believed that she loved her husband, in spite of how he left them, so suddenly, without warning. She tried to love everyone and forgive those who had wronged her.

Had she been right to keep the letters?

Jane slept on, showing no emotion, no movement. Marintha prayed that the words the Lord inspired the apostle Paul to write would reach into the soul she knew was present in this shattered body.

"Love does not delight in evil," she continued, "but rejoices with the truth. It always protects, always trusts, always hopes, always perseveres."

The words stabbed at her heart. After all these years, her son did not know the truth about why his father had left, and he blamed her for his leaving. In spite of her belief and love, she ignored the truth in sole favor of protecting her son, her boy, even at her own expense.

"Love never fails. But where there are prophecies, they will cease; where there are tongues, they will be stilled; where there is knowledge, it will pass away. For we know in part and we prophesy in part, but when perfection comes, the imperfect disappears. When I was a child, I talked like a child, I thought like a child, I reasoned like a child. When I became a man, I put childish ways behind me. Now we see but a poor reflection as in a mirror; then we shall see face to face. Now I know in part; then I shall know fully, even as I am fully known."

Tears filled her eyes. The mysteries of God—humankind had scarcely plumbed the depths of what could be known about the heavenly Father. With all the preaching and studying and interpretation in the world, no one really knows everything there is to know about God. No one ever would until the day when they meet him face to face.

"God knows you," she said to Jane, laying the Bible aside and taking up the brush and proceeding to smooth the young woman's silky hair. "He knows who you are. Not just your name, but who you are inside. Your hopes and dreams, what is going on inside your mind right now, this minute, even though you're locked away inside that body and can't let any of us know.

"And now these three remain: faith, hope, and love," she recited from memory. "But the greatest of these is love." Marintha put down the brush and adjusted the bed covers. "Someone out there loves you, sweetheart. I know somewhere someone's heart is broken. Still, I know eventually someone's going to come looking for you. Someone who knows you in this life."

Gathering up her things, Marintha squeezed the girl's hand. "Until then, know that I love you," she whispered. "That's something everyone can know."

EXCEPTING BRUCE, Janelle, and a waitress who wearily cleaned a booth on the opposite end of the building, the diner was deserted. It had been a popular hangout when they were teenagers, but the business had been through several owners and had lost its atmosphere. Bruce thought that going back to the beginning, where he and Janelle had met, would be a good place for a new start. Looking around as he stirred sugar into his coffee, he wasn't so sure.

Janelle stared out the window, her hands in her lap. Rain thrummed against the windows, providing the only music now that the jukebox no longer worked. Bruce looked at her, hard, for the first time in he couldn't remember how long. Laugh lines had begun to crease her eyes—at least he hoped they were laugh lines. He had them himself, although he couldn't remember the last time he had laughed. Her expression was downcast as he groped for words. A group of teenagers came through the door, their spirits high in contrast to the pouring rain. Drenched, they stood shaking themselves like a pack of woolly dogs, laughing loudly. Bruce and Janelle both found themselves smiling at the scene.

"It's been a long time since I've felt that lively," Bruce said.

Janelle took a sip of her cooling coffee. "I'm not sure that I ever have," she replied. "If I did, all of it's gone."

"I remember when you could out-hike and out-work me any day of the week. You were always so strong. You had so much . . . spirit. It's what attracted me."

She finally looked into his eyes. Bruce didn't like the sadness that greeted him. "You lost some things, too, you know."

"Yeah. I'm not sure what, though."

"You used to have an ease, a way about you that was always comfortable."

"That sounds exciting." Bruce reached for more sugar packets.

"You know what I mean. I knew what you were thinking. I knew what you would think was funny or outrageous. At some point, I couldn't figure you out anymore. You were so angry inside."

"That's interesting, because I don't feel angry."

"Well, you are."

"If I am, it's because you make me angry."

The small table seemed to expand as each leaned away from the other. Bruce held up his hands. "I didn't come here to argue with you. I came to see if we could salvage anything." This time he was the one staring out the window. "The papers came today."

Janelle pursed her lips. "You knew this day was coming."

"Not really. I had fooled myself into believing we could still work things out."

"Maybe before. Right now I think we're beyond help."

"Are we? Really, Janelle, are we?" Bruce watched the teenagers, telling stories in their animated adolescent style.

"Bruce, I have loved you for so long. I don't know how to make you love me anymore."

The statement took him aback. He remembered Marty's words. "I never stopped loving you. Not for a second."

"Then why did you stop showing it?"

Bruce ran his hands over the table. "I didn't realize I had done that."

"You did. That's why I asked you to move out. I couldn't stand you coming home—whenever you managed to get home—and treating me like I was there for the sole purpose of serving your every need. It was like you didn't see me anymore. You couldn't see my heart."

"I can't see something that's never shown," he said bitterly. "I could say the same thing about you. I felt like I was coming home to a robot."

"A robot?" Janelle picked up her purse and placed some money on the table. "I knew this was a mistake."

Bruce reached across the table and put a hand on her arm. "I'm sorry. That didn't come out right."

She laughed and pulled her arm away. "You call me a robot and then have the nerve to say it didn't come out right? You're farther gone than I thought." She sat for a minute. The rain outside had begun to slacken. "Why did you ask me here? You should have just gotten your lawyer to call mine. The paperwork's been set in motion."

"Is that supposed to mean there's no turning back?"

"As far as I'm concerned."

He ran his hands through his hair and sighed. Looking at her in the bright fluorescent light, he caught a glimmer of the eighteen-year-old girl wearing a bright pink mini-dress. She was still there, standing behind the transparency of time, waiting for him to ask her to dance. "This is going to sound weird, but I can't let you go without a fight."

"You mean we haven't fought enough?" Janelle allowed herself a tight smile.

"Can we go talk to somebody? Will you go with me to talk to somebody?"

"You mean like a counselor?" She sounded as skeptical as Bruce felt.

"Yeah. I don't know who. I'll ask around. I think we owe it to ourselves . . . and Daniel."

"Interesting. That's the first time you've mentioned him all night."

"This is about all of us, Janelle."

"I'll think about it."

"Think hard. Let me know."

Janelle walked out and got into her car, where Bruce noticed she sat for several moments before leaving. Between the rain and the streetlights, the glare was too bright to tell exactly what she was doing. But Bruce thought he knew.

She was crying. Probably crying as hard as he was inside. And he didn't know what to do about it.

MARINTHA SAT IN THE COZY DEN, her legs swaddled in a chenille throw, the fire blazing in the fireplace. Bruce had come in earlier, then left abruptly. She imagined that he probably had another date. He hadn't said anything after the first, and her imagination had run wild.

The whole situation between her son and daughter-in-law brought back too many memories—sad ones and bad ones. She rarely thought about Bruce's father, and when she did, the recollections only seared a place in her heart that she had hoped would heal with the benedictions of time. Only it never had.

She feared for Daniel, that he would face the same heartbreak Bruce had felt when *his* father left. And she feared for Bruce, for the heartbreak he would feel if he ever found out the truth about his own father.

116

The back door slammed, startling Marintha from her musings. Bruce came into the room and sat down in the other easy chair, flicking on the TV and muting the sound.

"I didn't hear you drive up," she said, pushing the throw to one side. "Did you have supper? I can make you something."

His eyes stayed glued to the set, silently tuned to *Monday Night Football*. "I had something."

"Where'd you go tonight? Working late?"

Bruce looked at her from the corner of his eye. "I went to see Janelle."

Marintha felt her heart leap but tried to control her response. "So what happened?"

Her son shrugged. "Not much. Another argument, some more hard feelings expressed. She served me with divorce papers today."

"Oh, no, Bruce, no!" Her hands balled into fists. "How could she do such a thing?"

"We haven't lived together for months, Mama. We all knew this was coming."

"You didn't try hard enough to work it out. Neither one of you." She reached for the remote control and snapped off the TV. "You should have gone to church, gotten involved in something besides your jobs. . . ."

"People who go to church get divorced, too. It's not a cure for marital woes."

"It may not be a cure, but it's good medicine."

"Well, if it's such good medicine, why didn't it help your marriage?"

"That was different, son." Marintha avoided his eyes.

"How? You're always throwing advice at me, but when I ask you what went wrong in your own marriage, you clam up like you're doing right now. Suddenly, you don't have a single answer."

"I'm trying to give you the benefit of my experience," she whispered.

"How can I benefit from your experience when you won't tell me what it is?"

"Because it is none of your business!" Marintha stood up and faced her son. Her grown son. "A parent does not have to tell a child everything. What happened between me and your father was between us; it had nothing to do with you."

"Well then, why do I feel like it did?"

Marintha turned away. "I never knew you felt that way."

"Well, you would if you had thought to ask."

She spun around. "I always cared about how you felt. You know that you could always tell me anything. Anything! I never did anything to make you feel it was your fault."

Bruce waved her off. "I'm tired, Mama. I don't feel like fighting with you. It seems all I do with anyone anymore is fight."

She backed away. "I don't want to fight about this, either. This is about you and Janelle, not about me and your daddy." She picked up the book she had been reading and went to the door. "If you want to talk to somebody, our minister . . ."

"I told you I didn't want to fight." Bruce's voice was quiet, even, eerily steady.

"Fine. I'm going to bed." She thought of something and came back. "I saw Jane today. Is there anything new on her case? Something I can tell the nurses next time?"

Bruce shook his head. "No," he said quietly. "Nothing new. Probably never will be."

Marintha went to her bedroom where she changed into her gown, picked up her Bible from the bedside table, and knelt, folding her hands on the faded quilt she had slept under for the last twenty years.

"Heavenly Father," she prayed, "I ask your forgiveness for whatever wrongs I have done in my life. I'm trying to show Bruce what he can do to save his marriage. I couldn't save my own, and it breaks my heart to see him lose his wife and child when there's no need or sense to it. Dear Lord, you can do all things. Please help Bruce find his way. Give him your direction and give him wisdom. Give me the courage to do what I need to do to make things right with him. In Jesus' name. Amen."

Marintha struggled to her feet and got into bed, where she read the Bible until she fell asleep and dreamed about her family together again, about life the way it was supposed to be.

WHEN HE ARRIVED AT WORK early the next morning, Bruce found a woman sitting in his office. She was ordinary looking, wearing a plain brown suit and sensible pumps, with a nondescript hairstyle. Average height, a little wide through the hips. An average middle-aged woman.

Yet what she proposed was extraordinary.

"I can help you find out who the missing girl is," she said matter-of-factly, as if she went around every day identifying missing persons.

"And you can do this how?" Bruce took out a legal pad and jotted down the woman's name: Delia Saperelli. He made a note to check for any criminal record.

"I have the gift of second sight." She sat back, expressionless.

Bruce blinked. "Second sight? You mean like a psychic?"

Delia shook her head. "I don't like to use that term."

"If that's what you are . . ."

"Psychics have gotten a bad rap. The media likes to paint us as weirdos out for publicity. I'm not like that."

"If you're not like that, then what are you like?"

"Interested, dedicated, ready to put in the time to help police solve their seemingly unsolvable cases."

Bruce leaned back and doodled on the pad, coloring in the triangles he drew. "What's your record of success?"

She leaned over and pulled a black notebook from a tote bag beside the chair. "You can read it all right here."

Bruce pored over the collection of newspaper clippings, most of them several years old. Murder cases, missing persons, lost pets, stolen objects—she had played a role in a variety of cases. Allegedly, he reminded himself. Everything was alleged until proven.

"What do you think you can do to help us here?"

"I understand you have no clues as to the woman's identity."

"No, we don't, but we haven't exhausted all avenues of investigation yet."

"If no one is looking for her, then you're quite hamstrung."

Bruce closed the notebook and handed it back to Delia. "Your scrapbook is impressive, but the King's Grant Sheriff's Department is not in the habit of hiring psychic detectives."

"You don't have to hire me. I consider this a mission, a calling from God."

There *he* was again, this time coming from the mouth of a woman he had only just met. "Ma'am, I appreciate your interest, but I don't think we can use your services at this time."

"You found some jewelry with the body."

Bruce sat for a moment, stunned. They had not released that particular snippet of information to the press or public.

"I'm right, aren't I?"

Her stare unnerved him. "Tell me more."

"It was a necklace. A gold chain with a pearl pendant."

She couldn't know that. Only the people who have had access to the body would know that. He had told only one other person—his mother—but Bruce knew she would never spread the information. That was one thing he could trust about his mother—she could keep a secret and keep it for good.

"Okay. I'll give you that."

The woman put the scrapbook back on his desk. "Study that overnight, and I'll come back tomorrow. You can decide if you want my help." She stood up and left before Bruce could respond.

Marty McGarrity had a strict rule about not using psychics, spouting criticisms derived directly from church. "They're all frauds," he had told his detectives and deputies. "I don't want anybody messing with the occult on my time. If I ever catch one of y'all using one, you will be out of here so fast you won't have time to collect your last paycheck."

Bruce was at a standstill. He had been over the evidence repeatedly, searched the Internet for missing women matching this woman's description. He had heard of many cases that police had solved with the help of psychics.

He put the notebook in his briefcase. *What Sheriff McGarrity doesn't know won't hurt him,* he thought, snapping it shut. *I might just solve this case after all.*

fourteen

OSCAR'S OFFICE WAS AS OPULENT as his home, spotless and luxurious; it was obvious no expense had been spared. Wanda and Derek waited anxiously while he and a secretary searched the file cabinets in the outer office for the rental application filled out by Kendall's neighbor.

Wanda berated herself for not seeing the connection sooner. Kendall had referred to the man repeatedly, yet she had dismissed the comments, believing what Mandy told her. Derek, however, had other ideas. Upon closer reading and examining the photograph of Kendall, he thought they should return to Rawlings to ask some more questions.

It was unthinkable to Wanda that someone could have harmed Kendall on purpose. Of all the scenarios that ran through her mind, she had not entertained the possibility that someone could have kidnapped her. The facts didn't fit. She had taken along a suitcase, her cosmetics, and personal items. Kidnappers generally didn't give a person time to pack.

"It doesn't make sense otherwise, Wanda," Derek had told her, trying to explain his suspicions that the neighbor had something to do with their daughter's disappearance. "If she had intended to visit one of us, we would have seen her by now. Nothing in these books leads me to believe that she would just vanish, leave a good-paying job and good friends to go off searching for goodness knows what."

Wanda disagreed with his theory but decided it wouldn't hurt to see Oscar again, to find out if he had anything new to add.

"Here it is," he said, returning and settling into the large burgundy leather chair behind the desk. "His name was Jasper Carney, originally from South Carolina. He was unemployed, but he had the money to pay the rent." Oscar rubbed his chin and studied the document. "Usually I don't rent to anyone who is unemployed. He seemed troubled somehow—I guess that's why I gave him a break."

"Did you do any kind of background check on him?" Derek reached for the report.

"I don't do background checks, Mr. Hunter. I guess I prefer to trust people whenever possible."

"That's a difficult thing to do these days," Derek replied, reading the application before passing it to Wanda. "I notice he didn't list any next of kin."

"He was an odd sort. Didn't like to talk about himself. The rent always arrived on time. I guess he must have been receiving disability payments of some sort. Direct deposit from his bank account. Although I have to tell you, it was hardly worth it when he moved out."

"When did he move out?" Wanda asked.

"I think it was about three or four months after Kendall disapp—" He stopped, flustered. "I meant to say, Kendall left. He came by one day and turned in his keys. I didn't see him. Just my secretary."

"What do you mean it was hardly worth it when he moved out?" Derek folded his arms.

"As my grandchildren would put it, he trashed the place. Full of garbage, filthy. It was a furnished duplex, and I had to burn the mattress, have the sofa hauled to the dump—you've probably never seen such a mess."

I have, Wanda thought, glancing at Derek, remembering some places she had lived and the lack of attention she had shown to housekeeping responsibilities when she was in the throes of a bender. She knew he had to remember as well; he was just too kind to say anything.

"Did he give your secretary a forwarding address?"

Oscar checked the file folder again. "No. Nevertheless, I am assuming that since he was from South Carolina maybe he still has family there or has returned there."

"Can we have a copy of this?" Derek handed the application back to Mr. Davenport.

"Sure." He went to the copy machine and returned in a couple of minutes. "I'm sorry. I feel I haven't been much help."

"You've helped just by knowing our daughter," Wanda said, grasping his extended hand. "At least you knew her better than we did."

He patted her hand. "You never know what life has in store. I know it doesn't look good, but she could still be found. Don't give up hope."

They left the office and got back into the car, where they sat quietly before Derek started the engine.

"I think if we find Jasper Carney, we'll find Kendall," Derek said.

"That's such a long shot. If we can't find our daughter, how are we ever going to find this man without a forwarding address?"

"I don't know. But we've got to put our heads together and think of something or else we might as well be trying to fly to the moon in a helicopter."

"If you think I'm crazy for the way I'm trying to find Kendall, then why did you waste the time and money to come down here? You never cared about finding either of us before." The words escaped her lips before she could think about what she was saying.

Derek tapped the steering wheel with his fingertips. "I did care about finding you, but you weren't so easy to find yourself. Always moving around, dragging Kendall all over the place, living with men who didn't care whether you lived or died or what shape you were in."

Wanda bit her lip, wondering what had happened to their optimism and good feelings.

"This is our punishment, Derek. Our punishment for all the wrongs we've ever done to our daughter and each other," she finally replied, her voice flat.

"Don't look at it that way."

"There's no other way to look at it. We've killed our daughter through our own negligence. It doesn't matter that she's an adult. We have killed Kendall. We have just gone and killed her." She jumped from the car and ran through the parking lot into the nearby woods. Branches scratched her face, and she stumbled over the vines that snaked across the muddy ground. Derek ran behind, calling her name.

"God!" she screamed at the overcast sky. "I killed my baby. I killed my baby, and now I'm never going to find her. I'm never going to find my baby." She dropped to her knees, where Derek caught up, falling beside her and gathering her into his arms. "I killed her, Derek."

"You did not kill Kendall," he said quietly, holding her face in his hands, staring resolutely into her eyes. "We did not kill Kendall. As far as we know, no one has killed Kendall. We have to believe that. We have to believe that she is alive somewhere, that she is waiting for us to find her and bring her home with us so we can tell her how much we love her and care about her now. Now, Wanda, now."

Wanda pounded her fists on her knees. "Why didn't I look for her sooner? If we do find her, she's not going to want to have anything to do with either one of us. I don't know why God even put me here on this earth. I've made such a mess of everything, and I don't even know what I'm supposed to do now." She gasped for breath. "I'm just chasing after air, chasing after some crazy ideal of what I want my life to be like."

"You can have that life, Wanda. You can have that life. You have to believe."

"Believe in what? In God? I've been trying that for a while now, and this is what he's brought me to."

"We've barely begun to look. This is just the first step. Haven't you heard that saying, a journey of a thousand miles begins with a single step?"

"I've already traveled a thousand miles, Derek." Her voice died to a whisper. "I don't think I have enough strength to take any more steps." She stared at the ground, barely able to see it through the tears that clouded her eyes. Leaning her head against her ex-husband's chest, she remembered other steps that had made a difference.

THEY WERE LIVING IN AN APARTMENT near the beach. It was a fair day, and they had decided to walk down to the shore, taking along blankets, Kendall's baby toys—and a cooler. Laying there, Derek drinking sodas, Wanda putting away a six-pack, Kendall had pulled herself up, steadied her pudgy little form, and walked straight toward Wanda until she toppled over, giggling. Their baby's first steps. Wanda swept her child into her arms, clinging to her, kissing her over and over, until she handed the dazed infant over to Derek so she could break open another six-pack.

THE REST OF THAT DAY was a blank.

"Wanda, it's fixing to rain. We should get back to the car." Against her will, Derek pulled her to her feet.

"Just leave me here. Let me die here."

He grabbed her and forced her to look him in the eyes. "I will not leave you to die here. God put you here for a reason. Maybe he put you here for this moment, the one moment when your daughter needs you most. It's time to quit messing around and get on with it, Wanda. You need to start living your life, and we need to find our daughter and bring her home."

"What right do I have to do that?" She refused to capitulate. "Why should I? She doesn't deserve me."

"Maybe she didn't deserve the old Wanda, but she sure would be blessed to know the new one."

Derek's words broke her obstinance. She looked down at the leaves and mud that plastered her jeans. "Blessed? You mean blessed out, don't you?"

Derek held out his hand. "Are you coming with me or not?"

She took his hand and held it tight. "I guess I better. Some-one's waiting on us."

"Yeah, she is. And time isn't."

"YOU'RE WITH WHO?" Mel sounded incredulous.

Wanda grasped the phone tightly and cleared her throat, which was sore from all her histrionics. "My ex-husband, Derek. He came down from Virginia to help me find Kendall."

"Are you sure that's a wise thing? I mean, it's been a long time since you was involved with anybody."

She hesitated. It was enough to deal with all the feelings that seeing Derek again had revived; she didn't have the strength to deal with Mel's prying. Mel was supposed to be there to support her, help her deal with the pressures of this situation. Over the last two years, she had been touched many times by his fatherly concern—now she realized she was as irritated by his curiosity as she had been by her real father's indifference.

"It's not like that. Our goal here is to find Kendall, not rekindle a broken romance."

"I've seen stranger things happen," he replied.

"Mel, the reason I called you was to check in. I didn't call for you to make me feel guilty about how I'm finding my daugh-ter, and most especially who is helping me find her." She didn't try to hide her annoyance. "I may be upset, but I'm not drink-ing, and that's all you need to know. I'll see you when I get back."

She hung up the phone before Mel could protest and felt guilty immediately. Mel had shown her nothing but kindness, and here she was slamming the phone in his ear. She sighed and flopped back on the bed, staring at the ceiling, deciding she would call him back later and apologize.

Motherhood had come as a surprise to her. When she learned she was pregnant with Kendall, she and Derek had rejoiced, but as the morning sickness hit and the realities of her new responsibilities became real, she panicked. Despite the doctor's orders, she drank throughout her pregnancy. Not a lot, just a few sips here and there, enough to take the edge off her anxiety. Soon she would have a child to care for, someone who would be completely dependent on her for everything. She had even convinced herself that she would stop drinking just as soon as their child was born.

The day Kendall was born, Derek reassured her that their daughter would have a wonderful life, that she would be the one person in their life who mattered more than anything. It was a miracle the child hadn't been born with any defects or syndromes.

The first time Wanda held Kendall, she was filled with a momentary peace, a moment when their ideal life seemed possible. She would put alcohol behind her, she vowed, get sober for the sake of their child.

Then the pressures began to wear on her. The sleepless nights, the endless laundry, the crying, the feeding times, the dirty diapers, the housework that she couldn't keep up with, the fatigue, the incredible weariness that overran her body and mind. This child, this demanding child, dominated her entire life, and Wanda felt as if she was fading away. Not since before the pregnancy had she felt like herself—the self she knew, the self she liked. The self that drank to distraction and then some, until she was free of pain and apprehension and anything felt possible.

Now Wanda sat in a motel room, the loving husband of that long-ago time now her ex-husband, asleep on the other side of the wall, the baby she had loved so much for a moment, missing without a trace. This was what her life had come to.

Sitting up, she opened the drawer in the nightstand and found a Gideon Bible laying on top of a phone book. Flipping through the pages, she wished she had paid more attention during Bible study at church. She had become a Christian only after becoming sober, and the life of faith was still new to her. The grace of God was a difficult idea to grasp when your previous life had consisted of grace coming from a liquor store. The crucifixion was even more difficult—the idea that one man hung on a cross, nails pounded through his hands and feet, taking on the sins of the world. Wanda tried to imagine the agony of all that, taking herself and multiplying that kind of pain and agony times millions and feeling the horrendous rush of the world's iniquities.

Jesus' words. The words in red. Those were the words that meant the most. Wanda ran her fingers over the highlighted text in the Book of Matthew. The word *seek* jumped out at her. She traced back and read: "Ask, and it shall be given you; seek, and ye shall find; knock, and it shall be opened unto you. For every one that asketh receiveth; and he that seeketh findeth; and to him that knocketh it shall be opened."

Wanda had learned early that prayer required asking. Her only problem was that she felt so selfish in doing so. She didn't think she would receive answers because she felt she didn't deserve them. Not after the way she had lived.

She knelt beside the bed. "Dear Lord," she prayed, "I guess this is where the rubber meets the road, as Derek would say. I believe in you, but I guess I haven't had much faith in you until now. I haven't had much faith in anything, especially myself.

"This time it's different though. I need to find Kendall." She took a deep breath. "I need to find her, whether she's alive or dead." Her voice broke on the last word. "Please don't let that be the case. Keep looking out for her, wherever she is. I'm putting her in your hands.

"I've sinned against you and against my husband and child. Preacher says when we come to Christ, we become like one of your children, and right now I feel about as lost as a child. I'm hoping you'll help me find *my* child, if that's what you want. I hope you can forgive me for what wrongs I've done, and I hope you can help Kendall forgive me, too."

When she finished, Wanda lay back down and stared at the ceiling, unable to sleep, ready to face tomorrow and the next day and the next, with whatever God chose to give her. She was ready to receive.

fifteen

COLD RAIN PELTED THE PAVEMENT as Bruce waited for Delia to meet him at the crime scene. After spending the evening reading her portfolio, he had decided the woman was legit. If the clips were to be believed, she could hold the key to breaking open this case. She had a history of providing clues at crucial moments, something Bruce found hard to ignore.

When he had called her that morning, she seemed eager to meet with him but was adamant that their meeting take place at the site. She insisted this was probably the last place the woman was alive, and her "spirit" could still be around for "contact." He was glad they were talking on the phone rather than in person so she couldn't see him roll his eyes. Skeptic that he was, at this point he was willing to try anything just to advance the case.

Presently Delia arrived driving a battered Buick with bald tires. She emerged from the car dressed in a bright yellow slicker, her hair covered with a crimson scarf. Bruce had hoped for something less flamboyant, more in keeping with the conservative image she had projected at their first meeting.

"Did you have trouble finding it?" He pulled his jacket up around his neck and shoved his hands into his pockets. "Of course not," he said, grinning. "I forget you're a psychic."

130

"No," she said flatly. "I recognized the spot from your stories on the news."

Bruce cleared his throat and led the way into the woods. Kelly had convinced her producer to keep the story alive and ran frequent requests for information from the public, repeating the footage of the body being loaded into the coroner's van the day J. J. finally reported it.

As they made their way to the site, the rain stopped, and thin rays of sunshine threaded through the trees.

"Would you call that a good omen?" Bruce looked over at Delia, who had stopped dead, her eyes closed and fists clenched. "Delia?"

She held up a hand, silencing him. She opened her eyes and walked past him, straight toward the clearing until she stopped.

"This is where you found her?"

"Yeah. Laying right where you're standing."

She motioned for him to stand back. Turning around slowly, her arms extended, palms down, it was as if she were feeling the air. Bruce leaned against a tree and chewed on a toothpick he found in his pocket.

Delia dropped her arms to her sides, and her head rolled toward one shoulder. "I came from somewhere else," she said.

Bruce didn't move, not knowing what to do.

"He brought me here and left me here," she continued, her speech slurred. "He did awful things. Awful things."

Delia lifted her head and blinked her eyes against the sun, which now shone brilliantly throughout the forest. As she walked toward Bruce, he could see that she had tears in her eyes.

"What did I say?"

Bruce repeated her words to her. She showed no expression.

"The first visit usually doesn't yield much valuable information."

"Well, you pretty much told me the murderer killed her here."

Delia nodded. "That's just a start. I'll do better next time."

"You mean that's all you can do today?"

131

"It takes a great deal of energy to contact the spirit world," she said, walking briskly up the hill, Bruce scrambling to keep up. She got into her car and rolled down the window. "When would you like to meet again?"

"Can you come again tomorrow?" Bruce was anxious to get on with it, and he felt deflated that she hadn't produced more solid clues.

"Perhaps. I'll let you know. Did you bring my portfolio?"

He rubbed his forehead. He had been reading it as he ate breakfast this morning, and it was probably still laying on the kitchen table, right where his mother was likely to find it.

"I left it at home. I'll bring it tomorrow," he called. Delia shot him an impatient look before she started the car and drove away.

Bruce headed back toward the office. When he reached the main highway, he noticed the Channel 3 news truck behind him, following him until he parked. Kelly got out and came up beside his window.

"Out pursuing a hot lead, Investigator Yeats?"

"A lead, but not very hot."

"Intriguing. Should I get out the camera?"

"Not yet. But soon."

He got out of the truck and walked her back over to the van. "You never called." *Of course, given the way I treated you last time we met, it's no wonder.*

"Called? Oh, about dinner." Kelly seemed taken aback. "Although I seem to recall leaving that up to you. Besides, I've been busy. You know, work and all. . . ."

"Too busy for an old guy, right?" Bruce grinned and put his hand on her lower back. She flinched, and he pulled away. "Sorry, Kel, I didn't mean . . ."

She turned and put her hand on his arm. "I'm sorry. I guess I've just been thinking about all this. You and me—I mean you're not even divorced yet."

"That's about to change." He looked at the ground before meeting her eyes. "Janelle served me with papers."

"So there's no hope—"

132

"Of us getting back together? I'd say chances are slim."

"But you're not saying there's no chance at all."

Bruce considered the reporter for a minute. Here she was, young and beautiful, at the start of a fascinating career that was probably going to take her far away from King's Grant within a couple of years at most. "It's not like you and I are looking at a lifetime commitment here. I think we're both just looking for a little fun, a little *diversion*." He rubbed the back of his hand across her chin. "Go out with me. Let's go tonight. *If* you don't have to work."

Kelly shook her head and smiled. "Getting together would be fun. Call me later?"

"I'll do it." Bruce leaned over and gave her a soft kiss on the cheek. She backed away and got into the van.

Going inside, Bruce thought about Janelle. The meeting at the diner had not gone well, and he hadn't talked to her or Daniel since. He was tired of thinking about it all—going to counselors, talking with Christian cops, and Marintha fussing over every little thing he said regarding his own marriage and his own child.

He needed time away from it all. Time with Kelly, a refreshing change. *Hang the rest of 'em*, he thought, heading toward his office. *It's time I had a break.*

THE BLACK NOTEBOOK LAY across the table. Marintha and Etta scrutinized its contents, alternately sighing, clucking in consternation, or spouting out exclamations over the outrageous claims they found among its pages.

"The gall of this woman!" Marintha finally cried, pushing away from the table and pouring herself another cup of coffee.

"Using the name of the Lord to justify calling up the devil's handiwork," Etta replied, flipping through the mass of newspaper clippings. "She claims her powers come from God, no less."

"What I'm wondering is what Bruce is doing with such a thing. I saw him reading that this morning, and I thought it had something to do with a case he's working on, but I just cannot imagine him calling on a fortune-teller what with all

133

the fancy ways they got of finding criminals nowadays." She quickly added three spoonfuls of sugar to the cup. "He and I are having us a prayer meeting when he gets home."

Etta laughed. "You want me to stay around for reinforcement?"

Marintha allowed herself a smile. "It might not hurt. Seems like nothing I have to say makes any difference at all with him lately."

The remote possibility of a reconciliation had raised her hopes briefly after he had seen Janelle, but since then, there had been no movement on either side. She hadn't seen Daniel since Christmas, it being winter with little need for yard work. And today was his birthday, no less. She had a small gift for him, but she hesitated to call. Janelle always seemed so abrupt toward her these days, as if Marintha were to blame for her family's breakup as much as Bruce.

In truth, her heart ached—for her son, her grandson, even herself. Bruce and Janelle had what she and Bruce's father never did—a complete home, a complete family. She thought about the box in the dresser and the letters inside. They explained everything, but Marintha kept them hidden, ashamed of her own lack of courage. Her husband had at least shown the courage to tell her son the truth. Only she hadn't let him. His actions had the opposite effect on her and made her more determined that her son would not know what kind of man his father had become, even if it meant that he blamed her for all that had gone wrong.

"Where are you?" Etta stood beside her, watching her absently stir her coffee.

"'When' is more like it. Thinking about when Bruce's daddy left."

"You don't talk about that much."

"Not much to talk about. I really don't like to dwell on it."

"I can see it's still causing you pain, honey."

Etta was right. It hurt just as badly as a fresh paper cut. "Some things always do. It seems like some wounds never heal up completely. It's only because of the Lord that I get through it, Etta."

"Amen to that." Etta turned back to the notebook, which she closed with a thump. "Now what you gonna do about your son and this soothsayer?"

Marintha picked up the notebook and placed it on top of the refrigerator. "I'm going to start praying for God to put a spiritual space between him and her. Then I'm leaving it up to the Lord to take care of the physical space," she replied, taking out the makings for a good old-fashioned pound cake. She thought she might need it to pound some sense into Bruce's head.

FLICKERING CANDLELIGHT illuminated the small restaurant located on the outskirts of King's Grant. Bruce realized he was glad for the dimness, because he was suddenly nervous about being seen with someone other than Janelle. Kelly sat across the table, dressed in a low-cut black dress that she seemed very comfortable with but that made him squirm—and not with admiration. Janelle had never dressed flashily, nor was she prone to exposing her body. Despite his previous preoccupation with Kelly's appearance, tonight he avoided looking at her.

"Is something wrong, Bruce?"

He allowed himself a glimpse, then looked down at his plate, sipping his tea. He had avoided wine in case the dispatcher called him out on duty. "Nothing," he said, laughing nervously. "Just a little self-conscious, I guess."

"Self-conscious about what?"

"Being here alone with you."

"We're hardly alone. The restaurant's packed."

Looking around, Bruce was surprised to find that it was unusually busy for a Thursday night. He noticed some people from his mother's church looking at him curiously; a couple of them waved, and he waved back, lowering his head.

"If you're embarrassed to be seen with me, then you shouldn't have agreed to this." The surliness of Kelly's voice took him by surprise.

"I'm not embarrassed," he said, raising his head and finally looking into her eyes. "It's just the first time I've been out on a date in years. Cut me a little slack, will you?" He leaned back and pushed his food around on his plate. He became aware of someone standing at his elbow. Thinking it was the waitress, he picked up his glass to ask for more tea.

"Hi, Dad."

Daniel, with Janelle standing right behind him. Bruce stood, placing his body between Kelly and his family, thinking that maybe he could hide what he was doing. Daniel sidestepped him.

"You're that reporter from TV," he said to Kelly, to her obvious discomfort. Bruce turned.

"Kelly, this is my son, Daniel, and this—" He gestured toward his wife. "This is my . . . this is Janelle."

Janelle nodded to Kelly, who did likewise.

"So what are y'all doing here?" Bruce wished the floor would open and swallow him.

"It's Daniel's birthday," Janelle said quietly, taking her son's arm. "You could have remembered."

Bruce closed his eyes and sighed. "It slipped my mind completely, what with the case and all."

"Yeah, I see 'and all.'" Janelle began walking away. "Say bye to your dad."

"Bye, Dad. Good meeting you, Kelly," Daniel said, gawking at the young reporter closer in age to himself than to his father.

Bruce sat again, crumpling his napkin. "Kelly, would you mind if we called it a night?"

"Are you sure? You haven't eaten."

"I lost my appetite."

Bruce paid the bill and walked Kelly out to her car where he kept his good-bye brief. He then sat in his cruiser and waited nearly forty-five minutes until Janelle emerged from the restaurant, followed by Daniel carrying the remains of his birthday cake in a small box. He followed them home, debating whether to stop or drive on. He decided to stop.

"Janelle!" he shouted as she entered the house. She turned and came back out, motioning Daniel to go inside.

"You two getting ready to fight over me some more?" Daniel asked sullenly. Bruce wished instantly he had driven back to his mother's.

"This isn't about you, Daniel," Bruce said.

"It's always about me. It's about all of us, Dad."

Daniel shoved his hands into the pockets of his baggy jeans. Bruce had called Mr. Hanks to check Daniel's progress, and the reports hadn't been good. He had continued sassing his teachers, and his grades had dropped even further. The principal also was concerned about the companions Daniel was choosing. Bruce supposed the low-key dinner was Janelle's way of keeping him from throwing a rowdy party that could lead to more trouble.

Janelle stood to one side, her arms folded across her chest. "You can't make time for your son on his birthday, but you can make time for Miss Bubblehead from Channel 3."

"Bubblehead!" Daniel cackled. "Good one, Mom."

"Go inside," Bruce said. "Your mother and I need to talk."

"What, and miss the show?"

"Inside, now!"

Daniel slunk off, glowering at them through the screen door before going to his room and blasting the stereo loud enough to scare away every squirrel in the neighborhood.

"That's it," Janelle said. "I don't care what you think about me, but you ought to at least think about how you look to your son."

"I do care how I look to him. I don't want to look like I'm rolling up and dying just because you and I don't live together anymore."

"Was I so awful? Was I so unattractive that you couldn't wait to put your hands on another woman?" The corner of her lip twitched.

"I always thought you were the most beautiful woman that ever lived. On the outside, anyway. But you haven't exactly been the most beautiful woman inside in a while."

"That cuts both ways, Bruce. I think something died inside you. The Bruce I used to know would never have forgotten his only son's birthday."

Bruce recoiled. *The way my daddy forgot mine*. The thought flashed through his mind, and he turned so Janelle couldn't see the hurt he knew had to show on his face. They stood in the yard, motionless, each waiting for the other to speak. Finally, Janelle sat on the front steps, resting her head in her hands.

"I can't do this anymore," she said.

Bruce looked at her and wondered where it started going wrong. "I don't *want* to do this anymore." He sat beside her and stared into the January sky, searching for the one constellation he knew, Orion, standing guard against the dark infinity. Only he couldn't see it. The night sky was so bright now from all the outdoor lighting that the stars were blotted from view. Bruce never imagined a day when he couldn't look up and see the stars. Yet here it was.

"I think we need to try a counselor," Janelle said finally, watching cars pass on the street.

"Do you really think it will do any good?"

"I don't know. Not if we don't try."

Bruce nodded. "Marty's been telling me about this group called the Christian Peace Officers. Says there's some kind of police chaplain in charge of it. He supposedly has years of experience with situations like ours."

"Have you ever met him?"

"No. I blew Marty off every time he mentioned it. Sounds like a nice enough guy."

"I thought you didn't think much of religion."

"I don't. It's not like King's Grant is a hotbed of psychiatric expertise, though."

"Guess not."

"You haven't heard about anybody at the hospital, have you?"

"No. They concentrate on people who are really sick." She laughed quietly. "Right now, we might fit that category ourselves."

"Might." He remembered his conversations with McGarrity. Bruce stood and faced Janelle. There she was again—that girl he met in the diner, half his lifetime ago. "I'll set a time and give you a call."

Janelle briefly outlined her schedule for the week. "We have to make this work. For Daniel," she quickly added.

"For Daniel," Bruce repeated, walking away and wondering how his life fell apart and how long it would take to put it back together again. He just hoped it was possible.

sixteen

SOME PEOPLE HAVE EYES like deep pools, mirrors to the depths of their being. Others have eyes as flat and dull as unpolished marble, impenetrable to scrutiny. It was one piece of wisdom from her father that Wanda had bothered to remember. She had seen both during this long day of searching. She found the store clerks, the managers, the servers with deep eyes to be the most helpful, allowing her to post the flyers anywhere on the windows or doors she could find a space. The flat-eyed crowd—they were another story. She might as well have been talking to stones.

As they traveled up I-95, Wanda fought against the potential futility of her search, hoping instead that someone, anyone, would see a flyer, call Mandy, who had volunteered to field the calls, and provide some bit of information that would lead them to Kendall. She and Derek had been at it for a week now, confronting skeptical police officers, indifferent clerks, and their own growing cynicism. They visited hospitals and spoke with harried emergency room nurses and apathetic receptionists. They navigated endless labyrinths of hallways and cubicles.

But no one knew anything. They just worked there.

Wanda stood in front of the day's last stop. She and Derek had parked at a grouping of filling stations, convenience stores, travel stops, and restaurants at an interstate exchange. Splitting up, Derek took a stack of flyers and veered off, leaving Wanda at this group. Entering the brightly lit store, she blinked her eyes. The sun had begun to set, and she found the fluorescent lights disconcerting. She was tired and hungry. Her feet ached from all the walking back and forth and standing around, trying to convince people to help her, trying to tease some bit of information out of these reluctant participants in her own domestic drama.

Taking a deep breath, she approached the clerk behind the counter, noting the name tag, which read "Bob." Appearing to be in his early twenties, he had the appearance of a bored college student putting in the time necessary for a paycheck to supplement the meager offerings from back home. Wanda handed him a flyer and asked if she could post it in the window. The store was oddly deserted for that time of day, so he studied the flyer, wrinkling his brow as he read the narrative and examined the picture.

"I saw her," he said, handing the flyer back.

Wanda, who had been casting longing looks at a beer display, was caught off-guard. "I'm sorry, what did you say?"

"I said I saw her," he replied impatiently.

"When? When did you see her?"

"It's been several months. I think she was in here more than once."

She grasped the flyer, suppressing the urge to jump over the counter and hug this boy's neck. "Are you certain? Now, can you remember anything about her—how she looked, if anybody was with her, exactly when did you see her—anything?" *Anything, please, God, anything.*

He took the flyer back. "She was with some guy. Tall, kind of wild-eyed. It was weird because he kept his hand on her the whole time. Like he was afraid she was going to get away from him or something."

Wanda pulled a copy of Kendall's photo from her purse, the one with the man in the background. "Does this look like the man?"

141

The clerk examined the photo. "It's too blurry. I can't tell."

"Look again." Wanda fought to keep her voice even. "Please. She's my daughter, and she's been missing for several months. We need to find her."

Bob looked at it again, leaning over the counter. Travelers began filling the store, and Wanda noticed a line had begun to form behind her. She could feel the next person's hot breath against her neck. "It could be. Like I said, I can't be sure."

She took the picture back. "I'm going to find my husband, and then we'll be back to talk to you some more."

Going outside, she realized she had called Derek her husband, although he hadn't been that in years. It was no time to parse words, though; finally, *finally* she had a lead. "Derek!" she yelled, before realizing she had attracted the attention of every traveler within a hundred yards. Covering her mouth, she ducked her head and trotted toward the car to wait for him to return.

Kendall had been alive after she left Rawlings, and she had been with someone. Someone had seen her. Only one person, but that was enough. It was enough to go on, to give her hope, to give her the strength she thought she was losing during this long, heartless week. Wanda paced around the car, her mind racing, wondering what they should do next, who they should contact, what their next move might be. Hugging the flyers to her chest, she wondered where Kendall was now, where Jasper Carney could be—was there a chance her daughter was all right, that he hadn't hurt her, harmed her— she wouldn't allow herself to think beyond those possibilities. She couldn't. She hoped God was giving her a second chance, and she didn't want to blow it by fabricating scenarios that wouldn't pan out. Ninety percent of what people worry about never happens. Wanda had heard that somewhere once.

She spotted Derek across the parking lot, walking wearily, his head down, looking dejected. Running toward him, scattering flyers in her wake, she couldn't hold it in.

142

"Somebody saw her," she yelled, nearly trampling an elderly couple who were trying to get back to their car. She dodged them and ran straight at Derek, who was looking at her in amazement.

"Who saw her?"

"A clerk, at that store over there." She pointed toward the convenience store.

"When?"

"A few months ago."

Derek's face fell. "Wanda, that could have been anybody. People's memories are incredibly unreliable."

She stood back. "I haven't come all this way to discount what he says just yet. After all the pep talks you've given me this week, I'm not about to let you do it, either. You're coming with me now, and we're going to ask him some more questions, and we're going to get to the bottom of this." Turning, she marched several feet before realizing Derek wasn't beside her. Looking back, she saw him standing beside the car, his shoulders shaking, covering his face with his hands.

The scene pulled her short. All week, Derek had been the strong one, holding her up when she was about to fall. Now, at the first sign of good news, at the first evidence of Kendall in the flesh, he had fallen apart. She went back and took him into her arms without a word, holding him until he drew away and pulled a fresh white handkerchief from his pocket.

"You know, that's my part you're playing," she said, rubbing his shoulder.

He laughed sheepishly, drying his eyes. "I guess I was more upset than I let on. I wasted a lot of time, too, you know. We all missed a lot, not being together like we should've been."

Wanda nodded. "I guess I never realized the burden you carried. I was selfish, thinking the baggage was all mine."

Derek looked around before meeting her eyes. "I know one thing."

"What's that?"

"If we don't pick up all these flyers before we go see that clerk, *we're* the ones that are going to wind up in jail."

WANDA DIDN'T SLEEP. Instead, she paced around the bed, stopping herself from running next door to talk to Derek. Their follow-up questions hadn't elicited any more information from the clerk. Derek had questioned him so intensely that Wanda wondered what kind of cop he would have made. All the clerk knew was what he had seen—it was a slim lead; she knew that. But it was just about their only lead.

The journals beckoned from a plastic shopping bag. Wanda couldn't stand the thought of leaving something so personal at home. They were the only objects that allowed her into Kendall's mind and thoughts. She picked one and began reading at the page where she opened it.

I have so many dreams for my life. I want to marry and have children. I don't want them to grow up the way I did, though. I want them to know that both their parents love them and want to take care of them. I want to own my own business and have it be a success, so I can be a role model for my children and a help to my husband. I don't care about being rich, I never have. Rich has a lot of meanings, and to most people that means pots of money. I want to be rich in the things that matter. Those things won't happen to me on my time, they'll come in the Lord's time, in the Lord's will. In the meantime, I have my plans and dreams and work and friends, and that's what makes me happy.

"Kendall was happy," Wanda whispered, running her hand over the elegant handwriting, wishing it could be her daughter's own hand.

Happiness was a word Wanda had to admit had never entered her vocabulary—not until she became sober, anyway. When she drank, she thought that what she found in all those bottles and glasses was happiness, but all it ever led to was misery.

She remembered the day she met Mel and he became her sponsor. Although she had stopped drinking a few months

144

before, she was having a difficult time and needed someone to help her stay focused. He related some of his experiences, including his own failures as a parent during the years drinking became his number one priority.

"I missed a lot of opportunities in my life, Wanda," he recalled. "I loved my family, but they lost their place when I had an important engagement with Johnny Walker or Jack Daniels. But the main opportunity I missed was the chance to be happy. Happy to spend time with my kids, happy to love my wife, happy to love myself and care about what happened in our lives."

Wanda had thought about his regrets many times, and when the time came to make amends, she knew she had denied herself that happiness as well. It cheered her to think that Kendall, in spite of everything, had learned the value of love and had developed the wisdom to make a life devoted to family, to work that meant something, and to the Lord, who had sustained her through her growth from angry child to mature and caring adult.

Toward daylight, she couldn't stand it any longer. Knocking on Derek's door, she wondered what he had spent the night thinking. When he finally opened the door, he was wearing a beat-up terry-cloth bathrobe over his pajamas.

"This sure looks like old times," she said. "Didn't you have that bathrobe when we were . . ."

"Married?" He laughed and scratched the stubble on his chin. "I'm not sure. I'm surprised you remember." Derek motioned her in and called for room service.

"I can't stand it, Derek. I feel like we're so close to her, but I don't know what we should do next." She flung herself into the upholstered chair next to the window while Derek perched on the edge of the unmade bed. "Should we try the police again? Should we go back to Rawlings? Should we keep going?" The sound of her own voice made her dizzy.

"I say we keep going."

"Why?"

"Because the police haven't been any help up to this point, and I don't see any reason they would help us now. Going back isn't going to get us any closer; not when we think they were headed north."

"But the clerk at the convenience store said he didn't know which direction they were headed." Wanda leaned forward.

"Doesn't matter," Derek said. "We're going on our gut feelings here."

Wanda sat back and stared at Derek. "When you talked with Kendall, did she say anything at all about this guy that lived next door to her?"

"No. All I know is what you know. What's in the journals."

She put her head on her knees. Derek stroked her hair as tears flowed over her wrists.

"If we're doing the right thing in searching for our daughter, then why does it all feel so wrong, Derek? Why does it feel like we're chasing the wind?"

"I don't care if you're searching for a person or the reasons of your own heart, uncertainty is a reality. We can never be sure of things, Wanda. We don't know if our decisions will be right until we make them and follow them through. That's what we're doing now."

She raised her head and popped a tissue from the dispenser on the bedside table.

"I say as soon as we eat, we hit the road." Derek answered the knock at the door, taking the tray of food from the bellhop. "We're already months behind Kendall. I don't think we can afford to waste any more time."

AN HOUR LATER they were standing in yet another restaurant a few miles up the interstate.

"She was traveling with some scuzzy-looking guy," the waitress, a woman named Nellie, said, smoking a cigarette while on her break. "They got some take-out. Seemed like it was mostly for him, though. She wasn't big enough to fight a flea. Only reason she stands out is 'cause she was a dead ringer for a cousin of mine out in Alabama."

146

"Do you recall when that was?" Wanda felt her hopes rise again.

"Last spring. Goodness knows, y'all, that's been ages ago. Why didn't y'all get her on *Dateline* or the evening news or something? They was talking about some girl the other day. I think she worked for somebody famous or something."

"We only found out recently that she was missing," Derek replied crisply. "If you don't have money and position, it's a lot harder to get taken seriously by those media types."

Nellie nodded, stubbing out the cigarette. "I know what you mean. Regular folks like us ain't got no, whatcha call it, clout, when it comes to getting bureaucrats to listen and get their rear ends in gear."

Wanda handed over the photo again. "Is this the man?"

Tracing the image with her inch-long, fire-engine red nail, Nellie squinted and considered for a moment before answering. "I can't see it good, but I'd say he bore more than a passing resemblance."

Derek took the picture and put it in his shirt pocket. "Do you recall whether the man said anything? Or the girl?"

"No. I don't think so. But I tell you one thing, that gal looked awful scared. She didn't look like nothing had happened to her, but she had that look that told you she thought something might."

"You didn't call the police?" Wanda was trying not to show her own fears.

"Honey, I can't be calling police on people just 'cause they look scared. People look scared for all kinds of reasons. Some people hate driving on the interstate. Some folks is scared of their own shadow."

"Did you notice what kind of car they were driving?" Derek would think of that.

"No." Nellie checked her watch. "Look here, my break's about over. I can't think of nothing else, 'cept to tell y'all don't give up. Sometimes things don't turn out as bad as they look."

They got back in the car. "I told you we were headed in the right direction," Derek said, turning on the heat. A cold front had blown in, and the north Florida air felt more like Pennsylvania's.

"Yeah," Wanda replied, pulling her coat around her and studying the map. "I just wish we knew our final destination."

seventeen

HER BEAUTY WAS HEARTBREAKING. The woman's face was unscarred, unscathed, delicately featured. Bruce stared at it until it burned into his memory. He wanted to run his hands over it so he could memorize it with his sense of touch, too, but he was afraid the oils from his palms would mar the surface.

Sheriff McGarrity, Morris Lund, deputies Kiley and Burns, investigators Starks and Wilson were scattered around the room, studying the model as if waiting for it to speak, to tell them her name so their torturous search could end. Morris had sent the skull of the unidentified victim to a forensic artist specially trained and skilled at re-creating faces. Bruce had read about the technique but had never seen such a model in person.

Soon the others left the room without comment, although Bruce could hear them talking in the hall. The room now felt like a funeral home, where the model had been prepared for visitation. Though the eyes were only glass, with blue irises based on speculation as to their color, they seemed to gaze at Bruce, wide and expectant, waiting for him to bring her back from oblivion, to identify her and tell her family so they would no longer worry.

He shook the thought from his head. "This would be a whole lot easier if we knew somebody was looking for this girl," he said, turning away and flipping through the case file.

"You're going to have cases like this, Bruce," McGarrity replied, turning the head on its revolving base, absorbing each detail. "It's amazing what forensics can do now."

"Yeah, but what difference does it make? We could show a picture of that model from here to Timbuktu, and if the right people aren't watching, what difference will it make?"

"The thing is, you never know when the right people *might* be watching." Marty sighed and motioned Bruce to follow him back to his office. "With all the police and sheriffs' departments out there," McGarrity said, relaxing in his leather chair, "and all the people involved in law enforcement, reports fall through the cracks, detectives fail to follow up, people lose track of their own loved ones for reasons only they know about. We can't worry about all that. We're here to do our jobs, Bruce—*our* jobs. Right now your job is to get pictures of that model and put it on every TV station and in every newspaper and on every web site you can find."

"It seems like I've looked at every missing person report in the United States. No one is looking for this woman. If they were, I'd have known about it by now. All we did was waste that artist's time."

McGarrity leaned back and studied Bruce for several moments. "I've seen countless people become jaded by this job, but I think you are about the worst."

Bruce blinked, surprised by his boss's candor. "I wouldn't call it jaded. I'd call it being realistic."

"Jaded, Bruce. When you lose your sense of duty, your sense of responsibility to people you've sworn to protect and defend—even when they're dead and gone—then you've lost sight of why you became a law enforcement officer. Now, do you want to tell me why you became a law enforcement officer?"

Bruce stared at the stacks of file folders that marched around the perimeter of McGarrity's desk like disheveled skyscrapers. He knew why, but he didn't want to say it. Didn't want to admit it.

He had become a cop because he wanted to find his father. By becoming a cop, he would have access to all kinds of investigative tools that he could use to look for his long-lost daddy, bring him home where he belonged.

Yet once he became a cop, Bruce became afraid—afraid of what he might find. Police work is about finding out the facts of a situation, but sometimes in the process, circumstances also reveal the truth, and Bruce was a man afraid of the truth, any kind of truth, about himself, his father, his mother, his wife, his son. Afraid of the mess he had made of his own life. Afraid of God.

Afraid of God.

The thought struck him now that he had never loved God the way his mother tried to teach him to because he was afraid.

God always knows the truth, Marintha had told him, often. *He sees everything and knows everything about you, Bruce. What you're thinking, what you're feeling. He knows your prayers before you even say them out loud, but he still wants to hear them from you, son.*

He looked up at McGarrity, who was still staring at him curiously.

"I didn't think it was such a hard question," the sheriff said.

"It's not, really," said Bruce, feeling like a kid being put on the spot by an overzealous adult asking him what he wanted to be when he grew up. He tried to think of something he thought McGarrity might want to hear, but nothing came.

The truth, Bruce. The truth.

So he told the truth. How his father left and never came back to see him. At the end of his story, McGarrity smiled. "So did you?"

"Did I what?"

"Find him."

"That's the peculiar part. I never bothered looking."

"Well, then, consider yourself assigned to a new case."

A look of alarm crossed Bruce's face. "I've got a desk piled almost as high as yours now!"

151

This time, McGarrity laughed. "Not a formal case. Look for your father. While you're searching for missing persons, you might as well add him to the list. Who knows? You might just find them both."

Bruce got up and went back to the room where the model sat on its turntable, watching him, begging him to find the rest of the missing pieces.

"I'm going to find out who you are," Bruce whispered, leaning over and staring into its eyes. "I'm going to find him, too, if it takes the rest of my life."

MARINTHA SERVED BRUCE heaping portions of steaming meat loaf and fluffy mashed potatoes before seating herself at the kitchen table. He dug in immediately.

"Could we at least say the blessing first?"

Bruce put down his fork and bowed his head without closing his eyes.

"Heavenly Father, we thank you for these blessings and ask your protection over our family. In Jesus' name we pray. Amen." Marintha picked up her fork, then noticed that Bruce was just staring at his plate.

"It tastes okay, doesn't it? It's the same recipe I've used for years. Maybe with a little adjustment here and there."

"Meat loaf's fine. I just have a lot on my mind."

"The missing girl?"

"Among other things."

"Have you been to see Daniel lately? If you see him, I have a birthday gift that I want him to have." Marintha pushed the potatoes around her plate, wondering when she had seen her son look so . . . so lost. It was the only way she could think to describe his expression.

"I'll try to think to take it after supper."

"After supper? You're going over there tonight?"

"No, I'm meeting Janelle. We have an appointment with a counselor." It slipped out. He hadn't wanted his mother to know about the counselor. Frankly, he didn't want to deal with all her questions.

Marintha felt her heart swell but squelched the rush of questions that formed in her mind. "I've never known you to call on a counselor for anything before."

Bruce laughed nervously. "I guess there's a first time for everything." He became quiet. "We thought we'd try it. Try and put things together."

It's about time, Marintha thought, passing the ketchup across the table. His next question startled her.

"Do you know where Daddy went after he left us?"

She nearly choked on her meat loaf. Wiping her mouth with a paper napkin, she fought to swallow the food, then put down her fork. "I thought you had put that to rest."

"You put it to rest. I never did." His voice was even, calm.

"It's not important where he went. What's important is that he never came back."

"It might not be important to you, but I have too many questions that need answering. I need to know, Mama."

Marintha picked up her half-full plate and put it in the sink. "What in the world kind of questions would you need to have answered after all these years?"

"Maybe explain why he left." Bruce was standing beside her now. "Do you know?"

Marintha couldn't speak. She had taught Bruce to tell the truth, *always* tell the truth. Now her moment of truth had come, and she couldn't bring herself to say the words, tell him why, explain what his father had done. "I don't know, son," she said, turning on the water to drown out further questions. Bruce reached over and turned it off.

"You know something, Mama. You just don't want to tell me." He turned and grabbed his jacket from the coatrack and left through the back door. Marintha returned to the table where she buried her tear-streaked face in her hands.

"Oh, Lord, have mercy on me, a sinner," she prayed. "I can't tell him. I can't disappoint him like that. Bruce's father became someone he doesn't remember him being. How can I tell him the truth, Father? How can I tell a man who's devoted himself to the law that his daddy died in prison?" She sobbed, unable to catch her breath, then lifted her head to stare at the moon rising over the trees, now visible through the kitchen window. Raising her hand, she covered the moon with it, blotting out the light, not wishing to see light when her soul was racked with so much darkness.

THE POLICE CHAPLAIN'S OFFICE was small but cozy, outfitted with two wing chairs and a comfortable sofa. Bruce sat on one end, while Janelle situated herself at the other.

Bruce had dialed the number six times that morning, hanging up after the first ring each time before summoning the courage to let the call go through.

Now they sat here, inside a church building of all places, the last place Bruce thought he and Janelle would ever find themselves. They had both attended church as children, but as adults they had strayed away, never even taking Daniel to Sunday school, although he had gone to vacation Bible school and to the occasional church camp. Marintha had taken him from time to time, but he always complained about getting dressed in a suit, so they didn't push him. He and Janelle weren't the dressy type either.

The chaplain, a retired police captain, now the Rev. Jack Mercer, sat in one of the wing chairs, a yellow legal pad in his lap, his hands folded on top. "I've known your mother for years, Bruce. I'm surprised that I have never seen you here with her," he began, to Bruce's immediate discomfiture. He had no idea that the chaplain was also the pastor of his mother's church.

"I guess I've never been much on church. Janelle, either," he added, glancing in her direction. She stared forward at the minister, smiling nervously.

"Many folks aren't these days, unfortunately," Rev. Mercer replied, shaking his head. "It seems the Lord has too much competition on Sunday morning. Although that isn't the only time church is in session."

"Well, I appreciate that," Bruce said, rubbing his hands together. "Honestly, Janelle and I are here about our marriage.

We've been separated for several months now, and it's tearing our son apart."

Rev. Mercer held up his hand. "Well, I suggest that, before we begin, we ask for a little divine intervention in this situation." He bowed his head. Bruce and Janelle looked at each other before bowing theirs, both keeping their eyes open. "Heavenly Father, we have two people here today who have come because they are obviously in pain and wish to have that pain go away. We ask your help and guidance in getting to the root of their problems and finding a way to put their broken family together again. Please let us all be amenable to your will and open to your saving grace. In the name of your Son, our Lord. Amen."

Janelle had yet to speak. Bruce felt awkward doing all the talking, but he thought somebody ought to get things going. Before he could open his mouth again, however, Rev. Mercer held up his hand.

"Before we get too far tonight, let's start by having each of you, in your own words, tell me why you are here and what you hope to accomplish during the counseling process."

Bruce cleared his throat. "I thought you were supposed to tell us that."

"I cannot make either of you make changes you do not want to make," the reverend said, pulling a pen from the coffee cup beside the phone. "You have to be the decision makers here. I'm here more as a facilitator, to help guide the discussion, help you set goals, provide ways for you to improve communication."

"Well, we can sure use some help with that," Bruce said.

"Janelle, would you like to go first?"

She seemed unnerved and wrung her hands. "I don't know where to start."

"Why don't you start with how you and Bruce came to be separated?"

"I thought you would want to start earlier than that. How we met and so forth." Bruce thought he read fear in her eyes.

"Well, that's important, too, but when a family is in crisis, dealing with what led to the present situation is more important than dwelling on ancient history, although that will generally come up over the course of our meetings."

Janelle nodded and took a deep breath. "I feel like Bruce doesn't love me anymore. I feel like he doesn't care about me or what I feel or do. We didn't feel like us anymore."

"What in the world is that supposed to mean?" An angry edge filtered into Bruce's voice.

"Bruce, let's let her finish. Part of learning to communicate is learning to hear what the other person is saying—what they are really saying."

Bruce leaned back and crossed an ankle over one leg, staring out the window.

"I didn't feel like we were a couple anymore. I used to know what he was going to say before he said it. But it was like he gradually cut me off. I tried to stay interested in his life, but it was like he didn't want to talk to me anymore, didn't want to tell me anything about his work or how it was affecting him." She laughed. "I guess I do know how it was affecting him, because he just gradually disconnected from me and our son."

"That's not true!"

"Bruce." Rev. Mercer leaned over and put a hand on his knee. "This is not the time to be judgmental. In fact, there isn't a good time to be judgmental." He pulled back and scribbled something on the legal pad. "So why don't you tell me what has happened, Bruce, from your perspective."

"She didn't want to listen to me anymore. Her job was more important than mine. Her feelings were more important than mine. It was like I didn't matter to her anymore. I didn't matter to my son either."

"Now that brings up something very important. How do you know that you didn't matter to your son anymore? Did he tell you that?"

Bruce considered the question, remembering what Janelle had said to him about the scrapbooks. "No," he said, hesitating. "It was just a feeling I got."

The chaplain nodded. "Now I want each of you to tell me what you hope to accomplish here."

Bruce and Janelle looked at each other. "You can go first," Janelle said. "Seems like that's where you always want to be." She folded her arms and looked away, seeming to study the books that lined the full-length shelves.

"I want to put our family back together. I want my life back."

"You want your life back."

"That's what I said."

"Life the way it was." The minister's eyes bored into his own.

"Yeah. No. I don't know." Bruce walked to the window and peered through a crack in the curtains.

"Janelle?"

"I don't want it back the way it was. At least not the last few years. I want it back the way our marriage was at first."

"And how was that?" Rev. Mercer prodded.

"We were in love. We didn't just love each other, we cared about each other. We cared about what the other person wanted and needed, and we cared about Daniel in the same way. We cared about what was best for all of us, not ourselves."

Bruce looked at his feet, feeling something he hadn't felt since he was a child—shame. Janelle was right, but he didn't want to admit it.

"Bruce, do you have anything to add?"

He shook his head.

"Then I think we have found a place to start."

"Really? How do you get that?" Bruce asked, aware that Janelle was now looking at him with a curious expression.

"It's a typical situation. Couples grow apart, and the wants of the individual gradually take precedence over the needs of the couple. What 'I' want becomes more important than what 'we' symbolize." Rev. Mercer motioned for them to stand and led them to the door. "Between now and our next meeting, I want you to write down ten positive things about each other. Remember the things that you love about one another, not those things you have grown to dislike."

"What's that supposed to do for us?"

"Hopefully it will put you on the road back to discovering what it was that brought you together as husband and wife to begin with. The two of you are like a house where a flood has washed the foundation away. We need to rebuild that foundation."

They walked to the parking lot where Janelle looked at Bruce for a minute before unlocking the car door. "He's pretty straightforward, isn't he?"

"Looks like it," he said, taking the key away from her and opening the door.

"Thank you," she said, accepting the key, their hands brushing in the exchange.

"You're welcome." He backed away and waved good-bye.

"I hope this works," he said to her retreating car. He made a mental note to remember to make the list. He didn't want Janelle accusing him of trying to sabotage the process. Too much was at stake.

eighteen

WANDA DIDN'T KNOW whether it was Thursday or Saturday—the days had blended so that now she didn't even care. The two sightings had led to nothing. At one rest stop after another, one travel center after another, the endless discussions with apathetic sales clerks and attendants had led to nothing. No one else had remembered seeing their daughter.

Now she and Derek were in another nondescript motel room, where Wanda lay across the bed, having flung her shoes across the room, and Derek stared out the window and drank a cup of black coffee. He had checked into his own room but came over to hers immediately after. Wanda guessed he was worried that she would run off to the nearest bar if he didn't keep an eye on her. Neither had bothered turning on the lights, and the mid-January twilight did little to brighten their moods.

She couldn't say the temptation hadn't been strong. Despite her affirmations of faith, her cravings dogged her, some of the worst she had experienced since she stopped drinking. God was near—Wanda knew that in her mind, but she couldn't feel him in her heart. Liquor had a real taste, real physical substance. She drank it and the feeling was instantaneous.

A few times, she had experienced that feeling after prayer, or in a worship service, but she was well aware that high was of a higher source. Caught up in the contagious singing and praise of her fellow congregants, inspired by the Holy Spirit, she felt God's presence, felt it in the marrow of her bones.

Those feelings were far away now. She stared at the ceiling, waiting for Derek to speak, afraid of what he might suggest, although she knew in her own heart what the next step would be.

There was nothing else for their search but to return home. Give up.

The phrase sickened her; it felt like Satan was muttering in her ear. Wanda had given up on so many things in her life: relationships, motherhood, jobs—at times even life itself. Giving up liquor was the only time she had ever been truly proud of herself. Her sense of self-worth had grown a little more when she finally decided to start looking for Kendall.

Now the search felt like another failed effort, another false start in a life full of false starts and unfulfilled promises. If only she could recapture her confidence. If only she could recapture that feeling of hopefulness she had felt the day she had stopped drinking.

SHE WOKE UP SOMETIME in the afternoon. The light from the setting sun nearly blinded her, and she hid her eyes, trying to blink away the glare. When she finally focused, she looked around and saw the mess her life had become. A strange man lay in the bed, passed out, his mouth open. Wanda had never seen him before in her life. Her belongings were strewn around the room, and it stank as if it had never been cleaned. The stench turned her stomach.

Dragging herself into the bathroom, she looked up and caught a glance of herself in the mirror. As she slowly fastened on the image of her face, she saw a person she didn't know, a person no one knew. A woman full of bitterness and sorrow, a woman who hated herself so much that all she could do was try to destroy herself inch by inch, day by day, until the pain left and she would be no more.

What happened to me? *she thought, leaning against the sink to steady herself.* What happened to Wanda Hunter? Where did she go?

She found herself screaming at her reflection. WHAT DID YOU DO WITH WANDA? WHAT DID YOU DO TO HER? WHERE DID SHE GO? WHAT HAPPENED?

Soon the apartment manager came in with the police, who carted her off to jail for causing a public disturbance.

It was the most hellish night of her life. Placed in a cell with thieves and prostitutes spouting profanity and shouting, she tried to stay in a corner, covering her ears against the commotion, but she felt as if she was being assaulted by demons. Only she knew the demons weren't really from without—they were from within.

As the guards released the women, by ones or twos or threes, Wanda welcomed the growing silence and for the first time in years began to look at the life she had led, the one that had brought her to a jail cell on a spring night in April, when the stars were shining and the moon was full. She vowed then that she would change her life and change it for good.

DEREK SAT ON THE EDGE OF THE BED now as tears flowed from Wanda's eyes.

"You want to talk about it?" His voice was gentle and understanding. She had forgotten that about him, that he could be so tender.

She shook her head. "Just thinking about the past again."

Derek held her hand and leaned over to turn on the lamp. She could see his crystal blue eyes, now surrounded by laugh lines, and the tinges of gray around his temples. "I've been taking a few too many trips there myself the last few days."

"If we had just—"

"Shh," he said, handing her a tissue and waiting while she dried her eyes. "We can't think about the what if's. The past is right where it is. We can't go back in time, Wanda."

She sat up and leaned against him. They stared out the window at the setting sun. "I guess we failed, didn't we?"

"I wouldn't call it a failure. There's plenty other things we can do. We knew this was a long shot, and we took it anyway. Who knows, if we keep going, we might still find her."

Wanda took his hand. "I don't believe we're going to find her. At least not this way. This was foolish."

"No, Wanda. Nothing you ever do for the sake of a lost child is foolish."

"I wonder why God picked now?"

"Picked now for what?"

"For Kendall to disappear. For you to come back into my life."

"I don't know. I'm not a preaching man."

"I don't think we have to be preachers to want to understand why God causes things to happen when they do or how they do." Wanda stood and pulled her suitcase from under the bed. She dried her eyes and began rearranging the clothes inside. "I need to go home."

He put a hand on her arm. "Are you sure?"

Be still and know that I am God. The voice again. "Yes," she replied, now packing with some urgency. "I need to be quiet so I can listen."

Derek looked confused. "Listen for what?"

"The answer to my prayers."

FACES WITH NAMES she didn't know, but a story she was growing to know quite well. As Wanda and Mandy surfed the Internet, looking at sites devoted to missing persons, the numbers amazed Wanda, the circumstances, the heartbreak that matched—or too often, surpassed—her own. So many young people, vanished without a trace. So many cases where the police lacked the one crucial bit of evidence that would put away the culprit. So many cases where the person had not vanished mysteriously but had simply fallen out of touch with friends and loved ones.

Derek had gone to a nearby motel to check in. Wanda thought it would help if they stayed in Rawlings where they could maintain contact with the last people who saw Kendall. Mandy had offered to let Wanda stay with her until they could figure out their next move.

As Mandy introduced her to the wonders of the Internet, Wanda wondered why she hadn't thought of it before. Here they could travel anywhere anytime, spreading the word about Kendall's disappearance with the click of a mouse. She chided herself for not being more up-to-date technologically but quickly dismissed the thought, heeding Derek's admonishment to let the past alone and concentrate on what they could do now, realistically, to search for their missing daughter.

Now Mandy was scanning Kendall's photograph into the computer, where she had designed a web page, complete with information on Kendall's vital statistics, the circumstances of her disappearance, and an e-mail address where they could be contacted. Soon Kendall's face appeared before them, beautiful and expectant, and Wanda hoped that someone, anyone, would find the site and have information that could lead them to her. She put her arm around Mandy's shoulders and squeezed.

"If I had only known what a wonderful friend you were to my daughter," she said, glad that Kendall had found a family to replace the one that had failed her.

"I hope you get the chance to know her, Wanda," Mandy replied, smiling. "She's the most caring friend I've ever known." She looked down at the stack of journals that sat at their feet. Wanda had allowed Mandy to read them in hopes that Mandy would pick up on something she and Derek had not. "The Kendall you've read about in those early journals is not the Kendall I knew. I think you can see the change as you read them."

Wanda had seen it. She picked up the last journal and turned to a page at random, one she had missed previously.

I know I've been hard on Mom all these years. I was so mad at her for drinking, but I didn't stop to think what might have caused her to become an alcoholic. I wonder sometimes that maybe if I had taken the time to talk to her instead of shutting her out, especially as I got older, she would have confided in me. Maybe I could have made a difference. I don't know. I could have tried at least.

"She took so much responsibility for things that weren't her fault," Wanda said quietly, handing the book over to Mandy. "I want the chance to tell her that she wasn't the cause of anything—not for me drinking, and she certainly wasn't responsible for helping me stop."

"That's the kind of person she was," Mandy replied, reading the passage before turning her attention back to the computer. She hit a few keys and plopped her hands into her lap. "It's done. Kendall's page is now officially on the Internet."

"What happens now?" Wanda eagerly watched the screen.

"We wait."

"Well," Wanda replied, taking back the photo that Mandy had removed from the scanner, "I sure have plenty of experience with that."

nineteen

DELIA SAPERELLI RAN HER HANDS over the clay model as Bruce nervously watched the door, feeling like a high school kid about to get caught smoking in the rest room. Thoughts of Daniel flashed across his mind, but he tried to push them away.

Other than the night of his birthday, he hadn't spent any time with Daniel since Christmas, and then only for an hour when Daniel stopped by Marintha's to pick up his gifts and drop off theirs. Marintha had begged him to stay for supper, but he had the usual excuse, that he had to meet some friends.

"This is a day to spend with your family," Marintha had told him.

"I see you guys all the time," Daniel had replied, gathering the colorfully wrapped boxes and bags.

"We hardly see you at all." His grandmother couldn't hide her disappointment, which Daniel failed to notice.

"There's plenty of time to see each other, Grammy. I'm only young once, as you always say."

And with that he had left. Bruce had tried calling him a couple of times, but Daniel showed little interest in getting together, even when he suggested a long-overdue camping trip one weekend.

As for Kelly, Bruce had gradually distanced himself from her, treating her in a purely professional and curt fashion whenever they met. She no longer came to the station every day; instead she called the duty sergeant for any breaking stories. Bruce found the fact that she no longer seemed interested didn't bother him. He had been foolish to let himself be tempted.

Now Delia stood in the office, doing her hocus-pocus, which Bruce now halfheartedly believed was his only shot at discovering the mystery woman's identity.

"She was quite beautiful," Delia said, holding her palms against the model's cheeks.

"Tell me something I don't know." Bruce leaned against the desk and folded his arms. "I need something concrete. Otherwise, we're both wasting our time here."

Delia ignored the remark, and when she finally spoke, her words only added to Bruce's exasperation.

"She was estranged from her family."

Of course she was, Bruce thought, *or else somebody would have come forward by now.*

"She had big plans for her life."

"Listen, Delia, I need to know something like her name or who did this to her."

The psychic put up her hands to silence him. Her eyes were closed as she concentrated on the model. "I believe she came from the South."

In case you haven't noticed, this IS the South. Bruce wondered why he let himself fall prey to this woman.

"I think her name might begin with a G or perhaps an N."

"Would that be first or last?"

Delia shook her head. Then the door opened and McGarrity walked in.

"Bruce, I need you to . . . what is going on?" He looked back and forth between Bruce and Delia, who had spread her arms and was breathing as if she had a chest wound. Hearing McGarrity, she opened her eyes, dropped her arms, and shrugged.

"I lost her."

"Lost who?" McGarrity asked, his eyes narrowing.

"Contact with the girl."

"Contact?" The sheriff let out a huge sigh. "Miss . . ."

"Saperelli. Delia Saperelli."

"Miss Saperelli, we no longer need your services." McGarrity stepped aside and held open the door.

Delia looked wide-eyed at Bruce. "But I was just beginning to make some progress."

Bruce took Delia by the arm and guided her toward the door. "I won't be in touch," he muttered, closing the door behind her.

"Bruce, I cannot believe what I just saw here."

"I can explain."

"There ain't any explanation, son. If I have drilled one thing into y'all's heads from day one, it is that I do not want anybody using psychics or fortune-tellers or voodoo or hoodoo in this job." His voice became louder. "We are law enforcement officers here. We look at the evidence and go from there. We go out and look for leads and clues. We never, never resort to using the occult to solve crimes, no matter how difficult the case."

"Police departments use psychics all the time," Bruce said, backing away. "I've seen it on the Discovery Channel."

McGarrity laughed. "Oh, you did now. Well, Yeats, the Discovery Channel does not run the King's Grant Sheriff's Department. I do."

"Listen, I was trying to do what I could to help find out who this girl is. You told us once to use any means at our disposal."

"Any reasonable means, Yeats." McGarrity rubbed his palm over his face. "Son, I don't know what's happened to you, but I think you need a few days to rethink yourself."

"Rethink myself?" Bruce wondered if that was something McGarrity had picked up during his own counseling sessions.

"You're not on top of your game here, and you haven't been for some time. It's not like you to resort to these kinds of things. You're trying to take the easy way out. I'm giving you a week's suspension without pay."

"What, are you sending me to detention?" Bruce smirked, not believing what McGarrity had said.

"Yeah, I guess you could say that."

"Listen, we've got a lot to do here. We have a stakeout with the task force tonight. You can't spare me for a week."

McGarrity left the room with Bruce in pursuit and strode down the hall toward his own office. He turned, and his determined expression drilled into Bruce's eyes like a wooden fence post into hard ground.

"We'll make do. When you come back, you better have your priorities straight, 'cause what I saw in there showed a lack of judgment, a lack of moral commitment, and a definite lack of ethics." He held out his hand, and Bruce handed him his gun and badge. "I'll see you in a week."

With that, the sheriff went into his office and shut the door in Bruce's face.

Bruce padded down the hall, avoiding the stares of the deputies and clerks who had obviously heard everything. He wished he could crawl into a hole and pull the hole in after him.

Until now, his record with the sheriff's department had been unblemished. He had received several citations over the years, including the state's Purple Heart for law enforcement officers when a drug suspect had shot him during an arrest. It was the one and only time he had ever had to draw his weapon and use it in self-defense.

Bruce had to agree with McGarrity. He had gotten sloppy, ignored the rules, lost his way—on several fronts.

After packing up the few things he would need on his enforced vacation, he went outside and watched the traffic passing by, all the people on their way to somewhere, oblivious to everyone else, involved in their own dramas.

Now it seemed he had one of his own. He never ceased to be amazed someone's life could come unglued with just a few reckless decisions—he confronted the results daily. He wondered how he had gotten so far away from everything he believed in, everything he used to regard as important.

Bruce had always believed in his job, his wife, his marriage, his son. For a time he had fooled himself into believing that he could solve a case with the help of psychic intervention and that he could still attract a woman half his age. Now he wondered if he really believed in anything at all.

MARINTHA FIGURED it had something to do with that psychic. Bruce had come home early with a box of his investigator's things and shut himself up in his room. After an hour or so she heard the stereo playing and wondered whether she should ask or just wait for him to tell her what had happened.

Two apple pies were baking in the oven for a fellowship supper at church that night. Marintha debated whether she should stay home instead and cook her son a comfort meal. The ringing phone interrupted her thoughts. It was Etta.

"Sister, you're going tonight, aren't you?"

Psychics aside, it always seemed that Etta knew exactly when to call her. She supposed it was the strong bond of friendship. "I don't know." She told Etta about Bruce's early arrival from work.

"I knew from reading those papers that woman was nothing but trouble," Etta proclaimed. "Now your son's paying the price."

"I wish I knew what to do for him. It seems like he's losing everything. His wife, his son, now his job." Marintha pulled a dishcloth from the closet and opened the oven door to peek at the steaming pies. The rich aroma permeated the room, and she hoped it would seep around the cracks of Bruce's door, drawing him out even if she couldn't.

"You know he hasn't lost everything. As long as he has you, he always has something."

"I know, Etta, but that's not enough. He's got responsibilities to other people. Bruce needs something to hold onto." She sat heavily at the kitchen table. "I don't know how he got turned away from God so. I took him to church while he was growing up, but it seems like time he got old enough to decide for himself, the decision was always 'I got someplace else to be, Mama.' Just like Daniel is now."

"Sometimes folks don't realize they have a need for something until the time comes when they really need it and figure out they ain't got it."

169

Etta's folksy wisdom cheered her heart. "You want to come over here and take a stab at him? Maybe you can succeed where I failed."

"You haven't failed anything, Marintha." Etta's deep, round laugh filled the receiver. "Don't you know this is all just a test? We don't get the grade until we're standing at the heavenly gates!"

Marintha chuckled. "Friend, you sure know how to put everything in perspective."

"That's why I'm here. Now, you coming tonight or not?"

"I'll be there. In fact, I'll pick you up."

"Praise the Lord. I done broke my glasses today, so that will be mighty welcome."

Bruce came into the kitchen as Marintha hung up the phone. He sat expectantly at the table while Marintha extracted the bubbling pies from the oven and placed them on cooling racks. She noticed he had changed into sweatpants and a T-shirt. "Are you going for a run?"

"Maybe. I am getting a little out of shape. Although the smell of those pies is about to throw that idea out the window."

She sat across from him. "What happened?"

"McGarrity suspended me for a week."

"Son, I am so sorry."

"Don't be. I brought it on myself." He folded his hands under his chin and stared at the tablecloth. "McGarrity says I need to 'rethink' myself."

Marintha watched his eyes. She hadn't seen him look so confused since the day his father left. "We all need to do that from time to time. We get to taking too many things for granted. Especially people, I think."

Bruce ran his fingers through his hair. He looked as if he was about to cry. "Yeah, Mama. I think I did that a lot."

Marintha didn't know how to comfort him. Their silence grew like gray fog over still water. "Maybe you and Daniel can spend some time together," she suggested, brightening at the thought.

"He doesn't want to spend time with me. He's got too much to do."

"Then you need to reach out to him."

Bruce thought, then remembered his assignment from the chaplain. He got up to go to his room.

"Are you going to see Daniel?" Marintha asked hopefully.

"Maybe," Bruce replied. "First I gotta make a list."

SITTING IN REV. MERCER'S OFFICE, Bruce scanned the list of what he liked about Janelle. They had assumed their previous positions on opposite ends of the sofa, but Bruce noticed she wasn't hugging the armrest as closely as she had the last time. *Progress is progress*, he thought.

Again, the minister opened their session with prayer. This time Bruce felt compelled to close his eyes. Although he didn't focus on the words, he wondered if Janelle had closed hers, too. Next thing he knew the prayer was over, and the reverend was asking who wanted to go first. To Bruce's surprise, Janelle volunteered, holding her hand up as if she were a student in a fifth-grade class, rather than one of three people trying to salvage the remains of a marriage.

"Were you able to come up with ten things that made you fall in love with Bruce?" He wore a bemused expression, which Bruce thought was odd.

Janelle unfolded the sheet of loose-leaf notebook paper and blushed. It was covered front and back with her precise handwriting. Even the margins were filled side-to-side. "It's weird," she said, laughing and smoothing out the creases. "Once I started, I couldn't stop writing."

Bruce looked at his own paper. He hoped it was a guy thing. He had barely filled the front of the page, although he had managed to come up with the ten reasons he fell in love with his wife.

"Bruce?" He realized Rev. Mercer was trying to get his attention. "Janelle needs you to focus your attention on her now while she goes through her list." Bruce folded his paper and laid it on the sofa cushion between them.

"I didn't know I was going to have to read this out loud." Bruce noticed her hands were trembling. "Of course, I fell for Bruce because he was good looking."

"Was?" Bruce smirked and ran his hand over his face.

Rev. Mercer smiled and readjusted his notepad. "I'm sure that you will both find that many of your reasons are still quite valid. Still, let's give Janelle a chance to complete her list before commenting."

Chastised, Bruce folded his hands across his stomach.

"He had a playful sense of humor back then, and he knew so much about so many different things. He loved and craved adventure nearly as much as I did."

Bruce remembered the first time they went rock climbing. After a long hike up the mountain, his date's verve impressed him. Not the least bit winded, she pushed him to continue, although he didn't want to admit that he was fading a little bit.

"If I can interrupt," Mercer said. "I notice that you even speak about yourself in the past tense. 'As much as I did.' Does this mean you've lost your own desire for adventure?"

Janelle studied the page for a moment. "I *still* crave adventure, but with my schedule and his, who has the time or the energy?"

The chaplain nodded and made a note. "Go on."

Janelle went on for several more minutes, listing small incidents, like the time her car had two flat tires and she had to walk a mile to the nearest house to call him. Meanwhile, he had happened upon her abandoned car and assumed the worst. A rookie cop, he had called out the force, fearing foul play, only to find that she was enjoying lemonade with an elderly couple who were glad to get a little company. She had loved that he cared enough about her to worry.

"Bruce, would you like to reiterate what Janelle just read to you?"

"Reiterwhat?"

"Rephrase it and repeat it to her in your own words?"

He gulped, not sure he had been listening closely enough. "Well, she fell in love with me because I was a hot young cop who liked climbing mountains and made an idiot out of myself when she went off and left her car without leaving a note."

Janelle's exasperated sigh told Bruce he had missed the mark. Bruce imagined they were probably the worst case the chaplain had ever seen, at least on the communications front.

"I see that is something we're going to have to work on," Mercer said, making another note. "Now you, Bruce."

Bruce made an exaggerated gesture of unfolding his paper and bending and unbending his arms until the look on Janelle's face told him he had better quit it—now.

"I fell in love with Janelle's sense of style, her playfulness, her willingness to climb mountains, ford streams, and leap tall buildings in a single bound, and the way she cooked macaroni and cheese," Bruce summarized, looking pleased with himself.

"The way I cooked macaroni and cheese?"

"Yeah. You cooked the noodles just right, no hard ones, and not too dry. The way my mama makes it."

"The ability of the woman to cook like the man's mother— if she was a stellar cook—is a frequently mentioned reason for falling in love," the reverend said.

"The way to a man's heart, you know," Bruce said, grinning, trying to tease one out of Janelle. She rewarded him with a sarcastic smile.

"Well, if you two chauvinists are going to make an issue out of it, that's the way I like my macaroni, too. I wasn't doing it all for him."

Mercer nodded. "That's a very important point."

"Juicy macaroni?" Bruce asked.

"No, that you do some things for yourself and some for the benefit of both. I have a sense here that while the two of you had many things in common initially, somehow over the years you lost sight of what was important to you, both together and as individuals."

Bruce mentally acceded. He couldn't remember the last time the two of them had spent time doing something together. He also couldn't recall when he had seen Janelle do anything for her own enjoyment. She used to have so many hobbies—crafts, reading those silly romance novels, roller-skating.

It went deeper than that, though—much deeper than macaroni. Bruce did not want to admit that he had failed at anything. It seemed lately that he was failing at everything. Watching Rev. Mercer write on his legal pad, Bruce wondered why he couldn't have changed sooner, why they had to sit here reading from silly lists instead of getting out of town like they used to do when things got rocky.

"Janelle, has Bruce ever been physically or verbally abusive toward you?"

She seemed startled by the question, and Bruce fought back a defensive response.

"No," she said after a moment. "Never. Although I don't know which is worse."

"What do you mean 'which is worse'?"

"Abuse or indifference."

"How do you respond to that, Bruce?"

"I never felt indifferent toward you, Janelle, and I'm sorry if it seemed that way."

She folded her arms and avoided his eyes. "Well, I guess I was doing the same thing."

"Rev. Mercer, if we keep going at this snail's pace, how are we ever going to put things right between us?" Bruce asked, perching on the edge of the sofa. "We have our son to think about. He's hurting, too."

"Then I suggest you bring him with you next time. We can get his perspective. I'm not just here for couples counseling; I also do quite a bit of family counseling, and I think that may be what is really in order here." Indicating for the two of them to bow their heads, he ended the session with another prayer.

"Heavenly Father, this man and this woman are seeking the people they once knew, the girl and the boy who fell in love many years ago. But their lives have changed, Lord, and time has passed. We pray your guidance as we search to renew that love and faithfulness between Bruce and Janelle, and we seek your grace on this family that seeks wholeness and truth. We ask you to bestow your many blessings on this couple, this family, as we do our part to heal the rifts that have driven them apart. In the name of your Son, Jesus Christ, we pray. Amen."

"Amen," Bruce said without thinking. Although he was quite surprised to find that this time he meant it.

Twenty

THE THOUGHT MADE WANDA sit straight up in bed.

What had happened to Kendall's mail?

Oscar had said Kendall's mail was piling up when he and Christine went to check on her. Yet Wanda hadn't discovered any old mail among her belongings. In fact, before she and Derek left on their search, they had looked into each box to see if she might have missed something by way of a clue.

She scurried into Mandy's room to wake her.

"What's wrong?" she said, bolting upright and turning on the light, which made them both squint. Wanda had been laying in the dark, unable to sleep, so it took time for her eyes to adjust as well.

"Did you get Kendall's mail?"

"Her mail?" She yawned and swung her feet over the side of the bed. "What's that got to do with anything?"

"It could be everything. It could be nothing. It just occurred to me that maybe she received a letter from someone or maybe there's a credit card bill—something, anything that might lead us to her."

"I don't have her mail. I don't even have any idea what happened to it." Kendall's friend was now wide awake and led the way to her kitchen, cheerily decorated with a bright yellow daisy motif, where she proceeded to make them both a cup of chamomile tea. After setting out a box of Scottish shortbreads, she joined Wanda at the tiny table, and the two stared into space.

"I'm going down to the post office first thing in the morning. Maybe they still have it."

"It sounds like a long shot, Wanda. You might be better off going back to see Darcy. Didn't you say she was still getting Kendall's junk mail? She may have gotten something else."

Wanda caught the weariness in Mandy's voice. "Everything about this has been a long shot. It's all I have left, but I don't think I would have had the idea if it didn't mean something."

Mandy smiled. "Kind of like the voice of God?"

"You could say that." Wanda thought back over the times during the last few weeks when it seemed God was speaking directly to her. Although she had heard of so many people experiencing such events, she wondered if it could really be true, that the Lord would take time to give individuals messages or to give them specific instructions about what to do about their lives.

Now she firmly believed it. Her previous efforts had come to naught, but she knew she had to keep listening, keep searching, keep trying. Kendall's life might depend on it. She knew her own did.

So many wasted years. Wanda sipped the tea and found it soothing. "I don't intend to waste any more time than I have to," she said. "I'm sorry I woke you, honey. You go on back to bed. I'll get this figured out."

"Are you sure?" Mandy could barely keep her eyes open.

"I'm positive. There'll be plenty of time for sleep later. I just need you rested so you can keep your eyes on that computer," she replied, guiding Mandy back to her room and going so far as to tuck her in and kiss her good night. "You're a good girl. I'm glad Kendall found such a friend as you."

Mandy snuggled under the covers and immediately fell back to sleep. Going back to the kitchen, Wanda found a pad of paper and listed all she wanted to do the next day. If God was going to give her the clues, then she had better note them all.

WANDA WAITED while Darcy went to find the bag of mail addressed to Kendall. First thing that morning, Wanda had called and wakened her to find out if she had saved any of it. Darcy insisted that it was mostly catalogs and junk, but Wanda did some insisting of her own, prodding the young woman to dig out whatever she had.

Now Wanda sat in her small den, trying to imagine what the room must have looked like filled with Kendall's lovely things. Her daughter had good taste, Wanda could see that, though she obviously had a great talent for thrift. The room must have looked like something out of *Victoria*, Wanda imagined, thinking of the times she had leafed through such magazines while waiting in line at the supermarket. Now the decorative items—the scented beeswax candles, the lace-edged scarves, the tin watering cans waiting for lush bouquets— were stacked in Wanda's spare bedroom, bereft of the life Kendall had undoubtedly given them.

Darcy returned with a plastic grocery bag stuffed to capacity. She handed it to Wanda and plopped into a brown corduroy recliner with tattered armrests. "I don't think you're going to find anything in there," she said. "It ain't nothing but a pile of junk. I was planning on throwing it out at the landfill next time I had a load."

"I know there might not be anything much, but I have to look to satisfy my own mind at least," Wanda replied, pulling out a stack of envelopes and peering into the sack. "You know how that goes."

"Yeah," Darcy said, sipping an orange soda. "I'd give anything if I could get in my old man's place and dig through his stuff and find out where he's throwing away my child support money."

Wanda scarcely heard her. In the midst of the credit card and magazine subscription offers, she had found a personally addressed envelope. It was thick and bore a South Carolina postmark.

"What you got there?" Darcy leaned forward with interest.

"I don't know, but it doesn't look like junk." Wanda pulled at the envelope. It was glued so tightly she couldn't pull it apart.

"Here; let me try." Darcy took the package into the kitchen. "Kitchen knives make real good letter openers," she said upon returning.

Wanda took the envelope back. "Thanks." She looked inside, then tipped the envelope so the contents poured onto the coffee table: a tapestry-covered address book with "Kendall Hunter" embroidered on the lower right-hand corner and a hard-backed book covered with bright yellow fabric.

A journal.

Wanda's heart leapt, and she wasn't sure what to do. She ran her hands over the books, afraid to open them, afraid of what they might tell her, yet also eager to find out if it was anything good.

"You want I should help you go through those?" Darcy asked, eyeing the books. "I don't know what you're looking for, but if you'll tell me—"

"No," Wanda said quickly, then apologized for her abruptness. "I appreciate your going to the trouble to look for these things." Wanda packed the mail back into the bag and hung it over her wrist, carrying the two books in her arms like a schoolgirl. "You've been so much help. I don't know how to repay you."

Darcy shrugged. "No problem. Just let me know if you find her."

Wanda smiled as she went out. "I will."

BACK AT MANDY'S, Wanda and Derek pored over the books, searching for answers.

"She talks here again about that man who lived next door," Derek said, running his finger down the page. "She was so trusting of everyone. Like she didn't believe anybody could be bad or evil." Wanda took it from him and read the passage:

His behavior is getting weirder by the day. I tried talking to him a couple of times over the past week, but he just looks at

179

me funny and mumbles words I can't understand. I tried to get him to let me come in, maybe clean up his apartment, but he just gave me this look, and it was like he suddenly got, well, like normal, and said he had a cleaning service coming and all. I hate to see anyone in so much emotional pain. There has to be some way I can help him.

She handed it back to Derek, who slammed the journal shut and threw it on the table.

Derek's temper had never been quick. When they were married, he had been the soul of patience until she tested him one too many times. Over the last few days, though, the strain had begun to test his composure. Where before he had been the strong one, now Wanda felt she had to hold herself together. This journey had not been only about their daughter—it had also been about putting to rest the unresolved issues of their shared past.

Each day, Wanda felt more like the high school kid at the dance with the cutest guy in school. Although the years had left a chain of evidence on them both, she still saw Derek as he had been. She knew that she was a better woman now. She could see that Derek was seeing that, too.

The mail lay scattered across the table. As Wanda began straightening the mess, her eyes fell across the postmark on the brown padded envelope.

"King's Grant, South Carolina," she whispered.

"Huh?" Derek opened his eyes and leaned toward her. "What're you looking at?"

"The postmark on this envelope. There's no return address or anything, but there's a postmark. King's Grant, South Carolina."

"Mandy!" Derek's yell startled her. Mandy ran into the room holding a dishrag and a dripping plate.

"What's wrong?"

"Did Kendall know anybody in King's Grant, South Carolina?"

Mandy stared off into space. "I don't recall her ever saying anything about knowing anyone in South Carolina."

"Jasper Carney." Wanda sucked in her breath.

"Who?" Mandy came and sat next to Wanda.

"Jasper Carney. Kendall's neighbor. Oscar Davenport said he was originally from South Carolina." She practically ran into the bedroom for her suitcase. Her heart was beating so hard she thought it might break her ribs.

After dragging the suitcase into the living room, Wanda started throwing clothes and toiletries around the room. Derek and Mandy watched open-mouthed. Soon she found the piece of paper she was looking for.

"KING'S GRANT!" she shouted.

"Wanda, what are you yelling about?" Derek took the piece of paper from her as soon as she stopped jumping up and down.

"Oscar Davenport said that Kendall's neighbor, the man in the photograph, was from King's Grant, South Carolina. Someone mailed this address book and journal back to Kendall from King's Grant, South Carolina." She was so out of breath she could hardly get the words out. "Derek, we've got to go."

She knelt and started repacking the bag. Derek knelt beside her and gently stilled her hands.

"Wanda, this could be another wild-goose chase."

"Well, then that goose best sit still, because I'm coming after him," she said, tearing her hands away. "I'm going whether you go or not. If you want to go on back home, then fine. If Kendall's journals wound up someplace where the man who used to live next to her happened to be from, then by God's grace I've got to go and see if she's there, too."

Derek rocked back on his heels and watched her work. Mandy sat on the arm of the overstuffed chair, observing the scene without comment. Shortly, Wanda stood and went into the bedroom, coming out with the rest of her things. She looked Derek squarely in the eye.

"Are you coming or what?"

Wanda was determined, and she knew he saw it. She, in turn, saw a softness in his eyes but held her expression, determined to do what she had to do.

"Mandy, it's been really sweet of you to put her up these few days," he said, giving the girl a hug before leading Wanda to the door. "We've got to run by the motel and get my things."

"Yeah, Mandy," Wanda said, kissing Mandy good-bye. "It looks like we're going on another trip."

Twenty-one

MARINTHA PACED the worn kitchen floor, wringing her hands. Bruce had become obsessed with finding his father, and the more hours he spent making calls and surfing the Internet, searching, the more agitated she became.

Truth will out. It was an old saying, and she fought against the knowledge of what she would have to do. Bruce would likely never trust her again now, though what she did had been for his own good.

Going into her room, she closed the door and locked it, something she never did. She had an irrational fear of locked rooms—she didn't really know why. Perhaps because if the door became jammed, the person inside would be trapped. She unlocked the door, then locked it again before going to the dresser and retrieving the box. Amid all the letters they had exchanged while they were dating, the letters she had sent to him in prison, and the replies she received, was one letter that broke her heart every time she thought about it.

Taking out the letter, she hesitated to pull it from its envelope. She had not read it in years, although it had become worn from the many times she had held it in her hands and prayed for its revelations to remain secret. Swallowing hard, she pulled out the folded pages, smoothed them on her lap, and began to read.

Dear Marintha,

I can only tell you how sorry I am for what I did to you. My betrayal of your love marked the end of my life. I have no life here in prison, merely an existence. Yes, I have jobs to complete and books to read, a chaplain to talk to from time to time. Still, nothing eases the sorrow of the pain I caused you and our son.

I'm writing to you now because I'm dying. They say the wages of sin is death, and I have surely died a thousand times behind these prison walls. I ask you to pray for my soul, as I do, and I seek your forgiveness, although I know that may be asking too much.

Enclosed is a letter for Bruce, explaining myself if such an act is possible. I hope you will give it to him when he is ready to understand what happened. I never meant to hurt him, Marintha. Nor you. I fell prey to temptation and destroyed our lives. I know God can forgive me—goodness knows you tried to teach me that with your faith. But I wasn't faithful to you or to God. If only I could forgive myself.

I love you always,
Fuller

Fuller Yeats had died in prison. All these years, Marintha had known where he was and could have effected a reconciliation for her son and his father, but she didn't want Bruce to know.

Now Bruce was on a mission. He seemed to think that if he found his father, maybe he could figure out what had gone wrong in his own life. Perhaps that was true, Marintha thought. She just couldn't bring herself to admit her culpability.

Hearing footsteps in the hall, she stuffed everything back in the box and stowed it in the dresser. The doorknob rattled.

"Mama, you all right in there?"

She straightened her sweater and opened the door. "I'm fine, Bruce," she said, smiling and pushing past him toward the kitchen.

"I've never known you to lock the door before." He followed her and began scarfing down peanut butter cookies from the newly filled jar.

"Can't a woman have a little privacy in her own house?"

"Gee whiz," he replied, crumbs falling from his mouth. "When did you get so touchy?"

"It's this search for your father," she said, moving aimlessly around the room until she finally planted herself in front of the opened freezer and pretended to decide what to cook for supper. "I don't like it. I feel like you're just going to get hurt."

"Well you ought not to worry about that, because I haven't found anything. It's like the man fell off the planet into one of those black holes." He nudged her aside so he could open the refrigerator to retrieve a soda. "His trail's about as cold as that frost you're letting out of the freezer."

Marintha closed the door. "Maybe he's dead."

"What?"

Marintha avoided his eyes. "I said, maybe he's dead. If he's dead, there's no one to find and no point in even looking."

Bruce scratched his chin. "You know, that's something I hadn't considered." He put the lid back on the cookie jar. "If he is dead, I'd at least like to know where he's buried. Maybe I can find someone who can tell me what happened to him."

Tears burned Marintha's eyes. "Are pork chops okay for supper?" she asked, trying to hide her fear behind cheerfulness.

"Great," Bruce said absentmindedly, wandering back toward his room and the glowing screen that was becoming Marintha's worst nightmare.

MAYBE HE IS DEAD. It hadn't occurred to Bruce before. He had always imagined his father was alive somewhere, living a secret life. When he was a kid, he had even made up stories about his father working for the CIA or the FBI to explain his absence to his friends. He was ashamed that his father had just run off without explanation.

The genealogy web site finally flashed onto the screen, and Bruce clicked on a link to the Social Security Death Index. If his father was dead, the index would surely list him, along with the zip code where he last lived. It wouldn't provide a specific address, but at least it would narrow down the area.

Typing in the vital information, Bruce waited while the search pulled up a list of names. Scrolling down, he found the name Fuller Yeats.

He had died five years earlier.

Bruce let out a sigh. For all his anger and need for explanations, he hadn't allowed himself any illusions during this search. He had been deluding himself about so many things and decided the time had come to stop. Now here was evidence that his father was no longer of this earth.

The screen seemed to waver before Bruce's eyes. *Why did I wait?* So much time had been lost, and now it was lost forever. He ran through the could haves, should haves, would haves—what they could have done together, what he should have done, what he would have said to this man he hadn't had the chance to see, to know. Time seems endless—until it comes to an end for someone who's important to you. Bruce knew that, had seen it too often on the job. If only he had applied that wisdom to his own situation.

Now he saw the years they could have spent together vanish with the click of a mouse. Going to the dresser, he dug through a drawer until he found an old photograph, one he had kept hidden since he was six. As he grew up, Bruce would take out the photo and hold it beside his face as he stared into the mirror, looking for signs of resemblance. Looking at it now, he saw it, the similarities that had eluded his scrutiny. He leaned the picture against the mirror, gazing at his reflection and wishing his father could see the man he had grown to be and was trying to become, hoping at least that his father would have been proud of his efforts.

Noting the zip code, Bruce clicked over to the zip code finder and read lists of numbers and towns until his eyes teared. He wrote down the number and made a note to resume the search later.

Turning from the computer, he pulled out the files on the unidentified women. He had attached a photograph of the clay model to the folder and now compared it with the photo of the comatose woman. The similarities were striking—the deep-set eyes, the dark hair, the heart-shaped face—if the artist's con-

186

jectures were correct and the reconstruction was true to life. Bruce tucked the files under his arm, grabbed his keys, and went out the front door without saying good-bye to his mother.

He drove through the streets of King's Grant, thinking about Janelle and Daniel, wondering what it would take to get the three of them back on the same page. They loved each other—that was certain. It was a matter of how they could find a way to get along and show their love. Already, Bruce could see it was going to be hard work.

As he approached the nursing home, a gust of wind threw waves of leaves across the road. The sky was low and gray, a harbinger of snow, although that was a rarity in the sand hills. He thought about the unexpected blizzard that had hit the state in 1973, closing the roads and interstates, trapping tourists and residents alike. Marintha had taken in a family from New York who had become stranded and subsequently spent the week ranting about the state's lack of snowplows.

Bruce had loved it, though. He had never seen so much snow, and a week out of school for weather? He couldn't dream of a better vacation. That was probably where his love of the mountains began. It was the nearest place to re-create that magical week. Bruce had slogged through the drifts and spent hours building massive snowmen and hurling heaps of snowballs at other kids from the neighborhood. Distinguishing where anything began and ended was nearly impossible. Houses, cars, shrubs—the snow buried everything, and Bruce thought it was the most beautiful sight he had ever seen.

Now he dreaded the idea. Although he had tried to stay busy, the thought of a week at home made him nuts. He wanted to get back out on the streets, look for some solid leads in his cases, get back to doing his job the way it was supposed to be done. Maybe the meteorologists were wrong about the weather forecast. When it came to snow, they usually were.

Pulling into the nursing home parking lot, Bruce found a spot near the door. He got out and walked purposefully to Jane's room, where a nurse was shifting her in the bed to reduce the incidence of bedsores.

"Should I wait outside?" he asked.

The nurse whipped around and placed a hand on her chest. "You scared me to death, Officer Yeats." She stood in place for a moment before resuming her task. "No. I'm just about finished."

"Any changes?" Bruce examined the monitors as if he knew what he was looking at.

"I'm afraid there's no change." She patted her patient's blanketed leg. "I sure do wish she had some family or somebody to come by. I know your mama comes to see her when she can, but that isn't the same somehow."

"I know. I've been meaning to come around more often myself, but I guess you could say that hasn't been high on my priority list."

"That's a shame."

"I know."

"Oh, I'm not talking about you." The nurse smoothed the covers and checked the IV tube. "I'm talking about how people get lost from each other. I have six brothers and sisters, and I know where every one of them lives, and I try to talk to them all as often as I can."

"I wouldn't know about that," Bruce replied, taking a seat in the easy chair near the window. "I don't have any brothers or sisters."

"Well, I guess if you don't have them, you can't miss them, but I tell you, if anything happened to any of mine, it would break my heart."

Bruce smiled and leaned forward to study Jane's face. "I'm not giving up on her."

"I hope not, Mr. Yeats. I'm telling you, you and your mama are all she has right now," she said, leaving him alone.

Bruce leaned back in the chair, wondering what his mother did when she visited. Did she talk to the woman? What did she say? The doctors said the woman still had brain activity, that maybe she could hear what everyone around her was saying.

"Did you just hear us talking?" Bruce whispered. "Can you hear us?"

He walked over to the bed and laid his hand gently on top of the girl's slender fingers. Someone, perhaps a volunteer, had taken the time to manicure her nails and embellish them with pale pink polish. They were beautiful hands that promised some sort of talent, a gift for caring.

"I wish you could open your eyes and tell me something about yourself," Bruce said, watching her eyes for a reaction, but they showed no movement. "I wish you could tell me your name. Tell me where you're from. Do you have a boyfriend? A husband? No, you wouldn't have a husband. You weren't wearing a wedding ring." *Unless the man who did this to you took it.* Bruce refrained from saying those words out loud. If she could hear, he didn't want to remind her unnecessarily of her ordeal.

If she came out of it. That was one of the biggest ifs. Maybe it was some small blessing that no one had found her yet. He couldn't imagine how he would feel if he had to watch Daniel in such a state. Although he would still be alive, somehow he wouldn't be Daniel anymore. He would be a soul trapped in a body, like this young woman missing the best years of her life.

"Dear God, please let me find out who she is."

Had that come from his mouth? Bruce shook his head. "Look here now, you've got to snap out of this," he said, laughing nervously. "You've got me praying here. It's gonna ruin my reputation."

A noise escaped from the woman's lips, and Bruce stared in awe. "Jane," he said, leaning over her face. "I know you hear me. Maybe God heard me then, too." *Dear God, please let her wake up.*

A minute passed, then another, with no more reaction. Bruce held her hand and brushed his lips across her forehead. "Sweetie, if there's any way to discover who you are, I'm going to find it." He stood back, put his hands in his pockets, and winked at her, even if she couldn't see him. "I might even give the old man upstairs another try."

He left the room too early to see the faint smile that passed across her sleeping face.

Twenty-Two

MILES UNREELED BENEATH THE TIRES, and Wanda fretted that Derek wouldn't drive faster.

"I'm gonna get a speeding ticket as it is, Wanda, and a traffic stop will just slow us even more," he said, exasperated at her repeated prods.

"Then let me drive."

"No way. We want to get there alive."

Wanda folded her arms and stared at the unending pine forests whipping past the windows. "We should have taken a plane. I knew it, we just should have taken a plane."

"We'll be there in a few hours."

"I don't have a few hours anymore," she shrieked. "I've lost so many years. I can't stand to lose more hours." She sobbed into her hands until she realized the car was slowing. "What are you doing?" Derek was pulling the car into a rest stop. "Haven't you been listening? We can't stop. We have to keep going." She pounded her hands against the dashboard.

Stopping the car, Derek put his hands on Wanda's wrists and stilled them. She tried to pull away, but his grip was firm.

"You have to get ahold of yourself," he said quietly. She stopped struggling, and he let her go. "We don't know what we're going to find when we get there—maybe just another dead end."

"I am not going this far to confront another dead end," she replied, drying her eyes and glaring at him. "If she's dead, I want to know so I can give her a proper burial. If she's alive, I want to take her home if she'll let me. I thought that's what you wanted, too."

"I do." He switched off the engine and draped his hands over the steering wheel. "I want to find her just as much as you do. I lost all those years, too, and I want to know what happened. But we have to be reasonable here, and if we don't keep ourselves safe and sane, we're not going to be any good to her if she is alive."

Wanda dug through her purse, looking for another tissue. "Why are you really here, Derek?" she said, lifting her head and meeting his eyes. "Why, after all these years and after everything I could possibly do to make you hate me, have you come all this way to put up with me again?"

He drummed his fingers against the steering wheel.

"Well, are you gonna answer me or what?" Wanda unsnapped the seat belt and turned to face him. "I don't know what all this means. I can't see why we're together here. Now."

"Because I never stopped loving you."

Wanda felt as if all the blood had rushed from her body. She stared at him, not knowing what to say.

"You asked," he said, running his hands through the temples of his graying hair.

"I did, didn't I," she replied, clearing the hoarseness from her throat.

"I didn't come here with any expectations of getting back together with you, Wanda, and that's not why I came. Not the only reason anyway."

"I know, Derek. I guess I just wanted to hear it." *Like the first time*.

WANDA'S PARENTS HAD NEVER TOLD HER they loved her. She couldn't remember them ever saying the words. She had been dating Derek for six months and had fallen, hard. He was so good—that was the word, good. Some people just have it down to their marrow.

191

No evil thoughts, no inconsideration, no pretensions. Derek was like that all the time, and she loved that about him.

One night as they watched the full moon rise golden over the trees in her backyard, he had turned to her and placed his hands on her face, turning it to him. "You know, I've never been in love with anyone until now." She felt as if her heart had evaporated, been sucked out through her skin somehow and was now floating up there, accompanied by the man on the moon. "I love you, Wanda. I think I'll always love you."

She had cherished the words, for they filled an empty place inside. Only they didn't fill it enough, because she hadn't found a way to love herself. And she certainly hadn't found her way to loving God, whose love is the fountain of all love on earth.

So HERE THEY SAT at a rest stop somewhere on I-95 in northern Florida, with Derek declaring his undying love. Wanda didn't know what to think, except that she must have been the stupidest woman on the planet to have let it slip away and the most blessed woman to have gotten it back.

"Now that I've scared you half to death, you want to go call your sponsor before we head on?" Derek was flashing her a cryptic smile.

"Oh, my goodness, I haven't called Mel in days." Wanda winced, thinking of how she had cut him off and had even forgotten to call and apologize.

She loved Mel—even though he was her sponsor and had to keep a certain distance; she had grown to love him for his wisdom. He acted the way she wished her real father had. He had been there for her often when the temptation to drink had threatened to burn away the new life she was building.

Derek's confession, though, had brought up something she had failed to realize until now. Her love affair with the bottle had concealed and ripped her from the other loves in her life—Derek and Kendall. And she was surprised to find that Derek's confession was leading her to one of her own that she could only now admit to herself.

She was still in love with Derek.

Now, however, wasn't the time to admit it, although she had pushed him into doing so. Their search for Kendall had to continue. Mel could wait. Derek could wait. Their relationship was mending as the days passed.

Kendall was waiting somewhere.

"I'll call Mel when we're done with all this," Wanda said, clicking her seat belt into place. "I promise not to backseat drive anymore if you can just get us to South Carolina today."

"Today?" Derek started the car and headed toward the highway. "It'll be midnight when we get there according to my calculations."

"Then I guess we better get some coffee," Wanda said, her voice firm. *No more true confessions today. Just get us to our daughter, Lord. Then I can tell him how I really feel.*

Twenty-Three

DANIEL SLUMPED on the couch's middle cushion, his arms folded. Although Bruce draped his arm over the back, behind his son's shoulders, the boy shrank away, as if trying to avoid all physical and mental contact with his parents. Janelle sat at the other end of the sofa, watching Daniel. Bruce wondered what was going through her head.

He had spent hours over the past week thinking about what had caused their breakup. While searching for his own father, he realized what a void his absence had created. No one to see him play baseball or teach him to drive or take him fishing or camping. And here he was in plain view of his own son and wasn't giving him the time of day. Bruce was disgusted with himself.

Rev. Mercer came in, took his usual place, and opened with prayer. Daniel didn't bow his head, so Bruce nudged him. Daniel shot him an arrogant look and continued staring out the window.

"Daniel, I'm glad you could make it tonight," the reverend began after completing his prayer.

"It's not like I had a choice. They threatened me."

"Oh? Threatened you how?"

194

Daniel slouched against the cushions. "Nothing specific. Just one of those 'or else' kinds of threats. Not that that means anything coming from them."

"Daniel . . ." Janelle tried to put her hand on his leg. Instead, he pulled away, walked to the desk, and perched on a corner.

Rev. Mercer adjusted his chair so he could keep all three of them within his field of vision. "Daniel, how do you feel about your parents' separation?"

Bruce shot him a look that told him to watch his language. "It stinks. They're my parents. They're supposed to stay together."

"Why is that?"

"Ain't that what marriage is supposed to be about? Together for better or worse or richer or slacker or whatever?"

"Yes. But sometimes people hit bumps in the road."

"The only bump they hit was when they quit paying attention to each other. Any idiot could've seen it. They only care about themselves apart from each other, and they sure as heck don't care about me."

"Daniel, you know that's not true," Bruce said.

"Then why don't you two try to do something about it? Instead of trying to work things out, Mom, you just throw him out, and Dad, you just leave without any kind of explanation, and suddenly I don't feel like I'm anybody's kid anymore."

The words felt like sleet, cold and sharp, and Bruce had to resist the urge to meld into the upholstery himself.

"When you lived together, what did you all like to do as a family?" The question was directed at Daniel.

"They used to be fun. We used to go camping, fishing, hiking, waterskiing."

"During regular times, how did they treat you?"

"Like parents. Don't do this, don't do that, who are you going with, here's your curfew. Now they don't care anything about my life. I could run off to California, and it'd be weeks before either one of them would notice. They were never home anymore, at least not at the same time."

Silence fell over the room. Bruce saw the tears glistening in Janelle's eyes.

"Rev. Mercer, what do we do here?" Bruce asked. "I know I haven't been a very good father lately. Or a good husband." He looked at Janelle before moving closer to her. "I guess that's because I never had a solid example to follow."

"No kidding," Daniel said, examining his bitten fingernails.

Janelle took a deep breath. "I want us to be a family again," she said, taking Bruce's hand. Her touch sent a surge of energy into his heart. "I think we all just quit when we should have worked harder."

Rev. Mercer nodded. "People tend to forget that marriages and families don't just happen on their own. It takes work— hard work—on the part of everyone involved. Parents, husbands, wives, children—all of you have your own roles, and too often parents become more like children as they reach middle age." He smiled. "No offense intended."

"I don't know if you'd call us middle-aged yet," Bruce said, "but I guess we've come to the middle of something here."

"I'd say it's the middle of a crossroads," the chaplain replied. "We are at the beginning of a journey. It seems you have been traveling the wide path, the easy road, for a long time, and now it's time to go down the straight and narrow path." He put his legal pad aside and motioned for Daniel to sit. Bruce noted that his son still wouldn't meet the pastor's eyes, but he did seem to be paying attention, at least.

"You know how people are always saying life doesn't come with an instruction manual?"

"Yeah," Bruce said. "I can't tell you how often I wished there was one."

"Well, there is."

"Really? What's it called, 'cause they need all the help they can get." Daniel smirked and leaned his elbows on his knees.

"It's called the Bible."

"No way," Daniel replied. "It's a bunch of old words written by some boring guys that don't make any sense."

"I think you'd be surprised at how relevant many of those 'old words' as you describe them are in our complicated world,"

Rev. Mercer replied. "I would say it contains the best advice available, all inspired by the one true God."

"But how are you supposed to know where to look?" Bruce asked. He flipped through the testament the chaplain handed to him. The rows and pages of words swam before his eyes. He couldn't say he was much of a reader, but if this could tell him what he needed to know, he was going to treat it like his next case and start out right.

"You start with the words of Jesus. They're easy to find because they're all in red."

Bruce found a page that practically bled. "Okay. But how is that going to get us all back living in the same house?"

"Just reading the Bible won't accomplish it. You have to do your part as well."

"So what do we do next?"

"How about you all plan a day to spend together as a family? Get away somewhere, maybe someplace you all used to go that has special memories."

Bruce nudged his son's knee with his own. "Daniel, where would you like to go?"

"Anywhere that ain't King's Grant."

After a few minutes of discussion, they decided they would drive up to the Welsh Neck Nature Trail. It was the perfect spot for a day hike, and the weekend was promising good weather—brisk, clear, and little wind to slow them. After a brief prayer, the three went out to the parking lot. Daniel took out his car keys and unlocked the door.

"Where're you going, son?" Bruce asked, putting a hand on his shoulder.

"Out."

"I mean specifically."

"You mean you two are taking all that garbage in there literally?"

"You said we didn't care about where you were going. We do care," Janelle said, standing firm next to her husband. "Now tell your father where you're going."

Daniel looked at one, then the other. "If you think I'm going in for all this God stuff and talking about my feelings and telling you all my business, you got another think coming."

Bruce stepped toward him. "Son, we're trying to start over here. We just need to know where you'll be. We may not be living together, but we're always going to be your parents, and we want you to know we care."

Daniel examined his keys, picking at the grooves. "I know, Dad. I just wish you'd quit bringing your job home and practicing it on me." He turned around and got in the car, leaving Bruce and Janelle staring at one another under the streetlight.

"Do you think this is going to work?"

"What? The counseling or the trip?" Bruce faced her and realized she was wearing his favorite perfume.

"Getting back together."

"It worked for a long time until we let ourselves get in the way. I always put my job first instead of you, and there will still be times when that's going to happen."

"I've been thinking about something." Janelle took a deep breath. "What if I cut back to part-time?"

Bruce studied her for a moment. "That would mean a lot less money."

"I figured it out. We could get by. Maybe not have as many material possessions, but we would still have enough to go on a trip sometimes, and camping doesn't cost us much. We don't have to buy a new car every other year, and you don't have to buy all the latest gadgets."

Bruce laughed. "I guess not. You seem to have given this a lot more thought than I have. That's not fair."

"No, it's not," she teased, grabbing his hand. "Still, if that's what it takes—"

"I promise to do better," he said, taking her into his arms. "That's a promise you can count on."

Twenty-four

THE TOWNS HAD BEGUN to look the same to Wanda, and King's Grant didn't seem any different. Strip malls and cookie-cutter subdivisions surrounded its decaying downtown, and its bedraggled appearance did little to raise her hopes of finding any concrete information. She chose instead to ignore the visual and concentrate on prayer, hoping God would lead them to anything that might tell them what had happened to Kendall.

Arriving long past midnight, they had spent a restless night in a chain motel near the interstate. Wanda could hear Derek moving around in the room next door and longed to talk with him, but she was afraid of her own feelings at this point and didn't want to have any close contact with him unless they were driving in the car or sitting in a restaurant. They were enervated from the journey and pressing forward on depleted adrenaline reserves.

When Wanda awoke at 8:00 A.M., she bolted out of bed only to become dizzy and fall into a nearby chair where she sat until the room stopped spinning. It had been a long time since she had felt that way; in a way she was relieved that her dizziness was the result of doing something she hoped was positive rather than a self-directed binge of destruction. She heard a pounding sound for several minutes until she realized it wasn't the blood in her head but Derek at the door.

"Wanda, you okay? I was knocking on the door forever." He looked at her and immediately steered her back to the chair.

"I'm just worn out," she said, barely able to speak. "I've come so far, and now I'm so tired I don't know if I can finish what we've started."

"Do you want me to go alone? I don't have a problem with it." Derek perched on the bed and folded his hands. "I don't want you getting sick."

"I haven't come all this way to give up. This is our last chance. If we don't find out anything here, then there's nothing left but to go home and give it up."

"I'm going to get you a proper breakfast," he said. "Don't move." He left her alone, and she took the opportunity just to sit and stare into space. She remembered a verse from Isaiah. It was one of the few verses she had memorized. "They that wait upon the Lord shall renew their strength," she whispered aloud as she slid off the chair onto her knees.

"Dear God, I'm running out of strength. I'm getting near the end here, and I'm praying that you'll give me strength to face whatever comes. I love my daughter, but I never showed her or told her. I came here to find out the truth, and I don't even know if I'm in the right place. I've waited on you, Lord, because I've been told your timing is perfect. It's hard living life on your timetable, and I'm doing the best I can. Please keep on teaching me what I need to know.

"Lord, if Kendall's dead—" Wanda stopped a moment and breathed heavily, wearied by her own pleas. "Lord, if Kendall's dead, I hope you'll show me what to do with my life. Show me when to wait for you. In Jesus' name. Amen."

Pulling herself up, she lay on the bed, hoping she could doze until Derek returned with breakfast. She didn't hear him when he returned with a breakfast he wound up eating alone, because he didn't want to disturb the peaceful expression on her face as she slept through lunch and supper and on through the chilly, tranquil night.

LOCATED IN A LOW, SQUARE BRICK BUILDING, the King's Grant Sheriff's Department wasn't exactly a lively place. Wanda clutched a stack of flyers as she and Derek approached the duty desk. A young deputy was holding a phone to one ear; she motioned for them to wait. It was Saturday morning, and Wanda had been livid to find that Derek had let her sleep for close to two days. Point of fact, she was angry with herself for not taking better care of her own needs so she could have the stamina to continue her quest.

The department was as quiet as the frigid air outside. When she and Derek had stepped out of the motel room, the cold had felt like an electric shock, something she had grown unused to during the mild Florida winters.

Finishing her call, the deputy smiled. "What can I do for you?"

"This is my daughter," Wanda said, placing a flyer on the desk. "She's missing, and we think a man from King's Grant knows something about her disappearance."

The deputy looked at the picture and read the details for several excruciating moments.

"Is there someone I can talk to?" Wanda asked. "I need to find her."

The deputy flipped through a notebook on the desk before picking up the phone. Wanda placed her hand over the young woman's.

"Who are you calling?"

The woman stared at her hand until Derek gently removed it. "You have to excuse her. This has been a very difficult time."

"I'm sure it has," the deputy replied. "I'm trying to call one of our investigators. I think he can probably help you."

"Wanda, let's let the woman do her job." Derek took her arm and led her over to an old couch, obviously a refugee from someone's redecorating project, sitting against the wall. They watched as the woman dialed first one phone number, then another, then a third, waiting for what seemed like hours after each dial. Finally, she hung up the phone, sighed, and walked over to them.

"I can't get in touch with him." She handed them a card. "His name is Bruce Yeats. He must have gone out of town, because he's not answering his beeper, his cell, or his home phone."

"Isn't there someone else we can talk to?" Derek read the card before handing it to Wanda.

"Everyone's out, either on patrol or on cases, or just off today."

"Great," Derek said, getting up and pacing around the room.

"It's okay," Wanda said, resigned. "We'll come back Monday."

"I drive like the wind to get you here, and you say we'll come back Monday?" Derek asked when they were outside again, Wanda pulling her thin jacket against the chill.

"God's timing, Derek," she replied. "First he lets me sleep for two days, and then the man we need isn't here. It's God telling us to wait just a little longer."

They returned to the motel where Wanda retrieved the last journal and address book from her suitcase. Kendall's address book was thin and contained few names, including the few friends Wanda had met. She noted the name of a dentist and a physician, along with a restaurant supply company.

"What are you looking for?" asked Derek, who had slumped in the chair and was surfing through the cable channels.

"I don't even know. Trying to learn something else about Kendall, I guess." She picked up the journal and opened it to one of the last pages.

Mama's been on my mind a lot lately. I should go see her and find out if we can have any kind of relationship, just friends maybe, even if she doesn't want to view me as her daughter. I always hoped that maybe someday she would come to me. I see now though that I may have to be the one to take the first step, even if it means more hurt. The idea that she's out there and I can't see her or touch her or talk to her like a daughter to a mother crushes my heart.

I was thinking the other night about the day I left Mama. I know it must have hurt her deeply that I didn't seem to care. I did. I prayed about it and put it in God's hands. I guess I

202

thought that my leaving would jolt her into doing something about her life. No one deserves to live that way. I hope she changed, not for me but for herself. Maybe my prayers made a difference.

They did, honey, she thought. *Only a few years too late.* She thought back to that morning. She had tried to remember it so often.

SUNLIGHT STREAMING THROUGH *the blind slats striped the floor of her bedroom when she awoke. The television blared—she had passed out, leaving it on as usual. Wanda staggered into the living room shouting for Kendall.*

No response except canned laughter from a sitcom.

Wanda went into Kendall's bedroom and tried to focus her eyes. Kendall had neatly made the bed and the closet door was open.

It was empty.

"You think running away is gonna solve anything?" she yelled to the empty apartment.

Going back into the kitchen, Wanda pulled out a chair and peered into the vodka bottle she had left on the table the night before. A couple of sips were left. Hair of the dog, she thought, feeling the liquid ease down her throat. "She'll be back," she said to a man hawking life insurance from the flickering screen. "She's run off before, but she'll get to feeling guilty and come on home."

She threw the bottle at the television but missed. The bottle landed with a thud on the shag carpet.

"You hear me!" she shouted. "Kendall's coming back later. She ain't gonna leave her old mama alone. She needs me just as much as I need her."

BUT KENDALL NEVER RETURNED. As the days passed, Wanda wandered the streets looking for her, then as now, wondering what had happened to her daughter.

"What goes around comes around," she said aloud.

Derek lifted his head. "How do you mean?"

"Here you are, back in my life. Here I am searching for my daughter just about the same haphazard way I used to when I was drunk all the time. Some things never change."

"You've changed," Derek said, smiling and reaching for her hand. "You care now."

Wanda nodded. "I'm trying really hard."

"You're not just trying. You're doing it." He grasped her hand and kissed it before turning his attention back to the television.

"Derek, when's the last time you had a good night's rest?" The bags under his eyes were growing more paunchy by the day.

"When I was twenty-four."

"Then you need to go back to your room," she said, pulling him from the chair. "I got my forty-eight winks. It's time you had yours." She escorted him to his room and kissed him on the cheek before he shut the door. "I've got a feeling we're going to need all our strength come Monday."

Twenty-five

THE LETTER LAY on the kitchen table. Marintha had just come home from Sunday morning worship and was mulling over the pastor's sermon about deception. He had taken as his text Romans 7, verses 21 through 23, and her mind had locked onto the words: "So I find this law at work: When I want to do good, evil is right there with me. For in my inner being I delight in God's law; but I see another law at work in the members of my body, waging war against the law of my mind and making me a prisoner of the law of sin within my members." If she could have an answer to a prayer in a sermon, she had received it that morning in the fourth pew from the front at Manna Methodist Church.

Marintha had tried to spend her life living according to God's Word, obeying its precepts and admonitions. This morning, though, she saw that in this area, in relating to her son, she had failed mightily. The information she had about Fuller Yeats affected Bruce directly. This was his father, for crying out loud, and she didn't think enough of her son to tell him the truth, no matter how much it hurt. Marintha realized she had been selfish and had put her own soul in a prison from which it now must be freed.

Bruce walked into the kitchen, yawning and stretching, and peered into the refrigerator. "What's for lunch?"

"I'm not cooking today," she said quietly, taking the letter from its envelope and laying it on the table.

"What, did you finally decide to retire?"

Marintha shook her head. "No; I lost my appetite at church."

"The sermon must have been pretty bad to cause that to happen." He snickered and removed a package of cold cuts from the fridge.

"Sit down."

He looked at her and saw that her face was drawn. Then he noticed the letter.

"Did you get some kind of bad news?" he asked, pulling out a chair and pushing the sandwich fixings to one side.

Marintha nodded, a sad smile on her face. "Yes. The only problem is I got it a long time ago, and I didn't tell you."

"Well, what is it? I can see you're pretty upset."

She reached down, pulled the box from her lap, and dumped the stack of letters onto the table.

"What's all this?" Bruce sifted through the pile without examining the details of the particular envelopes.

Marintha took a deep breath and avoided her son's probing eyes—eyes that had seen awful scenes she could not even imagine, scenes of what people could do to one another when filled with enough hatred and malice. Now those eyes were about to see the truth about her, and she worried that it might be the most horrible sight he would ever behold. Clearing her throat, she stacked the letters and handed them to him.

"They're letters from your father," she said. "Letters to me." She stopped and waited for the lump in her throat to go away. It didn't. "And letters to you."

Bruce took the bundle and set it down carefully so the letters wouldn't topple. "When did you get these?"

"I've had them for some time."

He examined the return address and postmark. "These are from a prison."

"Yes."

"Was he working there?" Even as he asked the question, Bruce feared the answer.

206

Shaking her head, Marintha put her hand over his. "He was an inmate."

An azalea branch scratched the kitchen window as if trying to escape the cold.

"What did he do?" Bruce laid the letter down.

"He killed a man."

Standing up so suddenly the chair overturned, Bruce paced around the kitchen. "Didn't you think it might be important to tell me, a law enforcement officer, that my own father had violated that law in the worst way possible?" He put his hands on his hips and stared at the floor. "Didn't you think I had a right to know? I mean, I asked you and asked you, and you never told me anything."

"How do you tell your son his father was an adulterer and a murderer?" Her voice shook not so much with fear but with suppressed rage. "How do you expect your son to react to something like that? How can I ask you to forgive your father when I've had so much trouble forgiving him myself?"

"I had a right to the truth."

"I'm telling you now."

Bruce set the chair aright and dropped into it. "Mama, start from the beginning and tell me what happened."

Marintha went over to the stove and turned the burner on under the kettle. "Your father was a traveling salesman—insurance. But you know that part."

"Yeah, I do know that." He fought to keep the outrage from showing.

"He met a woman in Tennessee. He fell in love with her, but she was married." She turned so she couldn't see his face. "She was a demon. She convinced your father to kill her husband so they could collect the insurance money. He knew how to doctor the policy so they could get more."

"Don't make excuses for him." Bruce stared at her back. "So he killed the husband . . ."

"They got caught." She returned to the table and shuffled through the letters until she found the last one. Holding it out to her son, she finally looked into his eyes and realized they were filled with tears.

"I don't want to read it."

"You have to."

"I don't have to do anything."

"Bruce, I told you this today because I couldn't bear to carry this anymore. I'm not telling you this to burden you. But you wanted the truth, so I am telling you the truth."

He snatched the letter away and read it quickly before throwing it back on the pile. "So I'm just supposed to forgive him."

Marintha went over to her son and placed an arm around his shoulders. He tried to push her away, but she held firm. "Listen to me," she said. "I've forgiven him, but it has taken me a long, long time to do it. Sometimes I think I never really have, but then I realize I don't have any anger toward him anymore.

"Bruce, forgiveness is something we do as much for ourselves as for the other person. It helps them to know before they die that we forgive them, that we no longer harbor anger or vengeance against them. We have to do it for ourselves, because the only way we can be truly close to God is if we let those feelings go and get on with the business of living." She paused to let her words sink in. "You have been so angry for so long, and I'm partly responsible. I ask you now to forgive me. You're a parent, and you know what it's like not to want your child to think less of you because of your own weaknesses."

Bruce avoided her eyes, knowing what she said was true, although he had not always been as ashamed as he should have been of some actions he had taken since he and Janelle had separated. "I can forgive you, Mama, but I don't know if I can forgive him for leaving us." He banged his hand against the table. "He left me! He left me alone."

"Son, people are always going to come and go in your life. But God is with us always." She rubbed his shoulder. "You know how you're always saying that you're working on a tough case? Well, the toughest case you are ever going to have is you, because that's a case that you will never solve. God is constantly revealing us to ourselves, and if we don't pay atten-

208

tion and learn from those revelations and take what we learn into our daily lives, then we might as well pull up a porch rocker, sit down, and quit right now."

Bruce couldn't argue with her logic—or her theology, wishing now he had a little bit of that himself. "Mama, I'm not sure what it is I'm supposed to be doing."

The teakettle whistled, and she bustled to turn it off before returning to the table. "Is that counselor helping you at all?"

Bruce shrugged. "Yeah. Some. Maybe." He had learned that he still loved his wife and that she still loved him, and they shared a desire to put their family back together. "I am learning a few things."

"Is he showing you where to look for the answers?"

The Bible. The counselor had described it as life's instruction manual. "Yeah."

"Then you're not lost. You're just getting on the right road."

If I can keep from making so many wrong turns, he thought, taking the letters to his room where he spent the rest of the afternoon getting to know his father.

Twenty-six

BRUCE SCANNED THE PHOTOGRAPH of Kendall, trying not to show any signs of recognition. Wanda refused to sit and instead wandered around his office reading the citations that covered the walls.

When Bruce opened his desk drawer, pulled out a thick notebook, and dropped it on the desk, the loud thump startled Wanda. Although she had finally caught up with her sleep, she still felt edgy, like she had a caffeine buzz, but she had made a point to stick to water and fruit juice. Bruce opened the book and turned it around.

A photo of a woman laying in a hospital bed greeted Wanda. She picked up the book and held it in both hands, trying to discern the woman's features. In a vague way, she looked like Kendall—the dark hair, the slender build—but something was different.

"Who is this?" Wanda asked.

Bruce's hopes fell. "It's a woman we found several months ago. She was badly beaten; she's been in a coma ever since. We haven't learned her identity." He came around the desk. "Are you sure this isn't your daughter?"

Wanda shook her head. "I don't know if I could really say unless I saw her in person." She handed the notebook to Derek, who stared at the picture, comparing it with their daughter's photograph.

"I don't believe it's her," he said finally to Wanda, who stared at the floor.

Bruce wasn't sure what to do now. It was his first morning back, and he hadn't expected such a big break on a case. He knew they needed to look at the clay model, but he could see that Wanda was emotionally fragile. The two had related the details of their search, and Bruce knew it must have been an ordeal, full of emotional highs and lows; he inwardly condemned the police officer who had spurned Wanda's pleas for help. Missing adult children were rarely a priority for police departments, and Wanda had been an unfortunate victim of the system.

When Bruce spoke again, it was with as much care as he could summon. "Several months after we found this woman, we found another one."

"Another woman?" Wanda turned her face up to him expectantly, and her expression nearly broke Bruce's heart. Derek reached over and took her hand, his face tight with apprehension. "Does she look like Kendall?" Wanda stood in front of Bruce, so close he could smell the scent of the soap she used that morning.

Bruce tried not to let his emotions replace his professionalism. He had done that too often in recent months, and he didn't want to do anything that would increase the grief of these two, although he knew he was about to tell them the worst news of their lives. "Mrs. Hunter, Mr. Hunter, the second woman wasn't alive when we found her."

He saw the anticipation on Wanda's face fade as she sank into the chair. For her part, Wanda found that her mind had gone blank, and she lost her ability to speak.

"Were you able to identify her?" Derek put his hand on her shoulder.

"No," Bruce answered. "In fact, there wasn't much to identify. I'm sorry to say it so bluntly, but the body was badly decomposed."

211

Derek became skeptical. "Then how do you know whether it's a man or a woman?"

"Our medical examiner autopsied the remains and discovered it was the body of a woman. Then our forensic artist took over and put together a reconstruction of what they think the woman looked like." He looked at Wanda, who still refused to meet his eyes. "If you think you're up to it, I can show it to you."

"I want to see that woman," Wanda said.

"Okay, if you'll step this—"

"Not that one," she said, putting her hand on Bruce's arm. "The one in the coma. I want to see her in person. I want to know for sure she's not my Kendall before I go looking at somebody's idea of what somebody might have looked like."

Bruce nodded. "That's only fair," he said, going to the door. "I'll take you over to the nursing home myself."

"She's in a nursing home? Why isn't she in a hospital?" Wanda demanded.

"The hospital could only keep her for a certain length of time. Once her wounds healed, they thought it best she stay in a facility where she could have the proper care for her condition."

Derek and Wanda followed Bruce to his cruiser. They sat in the backseat on the way to the facility, and no one spoke. Bruce knew the time wasn't appropriate for small talk, and he didn't want to deepen the wounds.

When they arrived, he went in ahead of them and spoke to the head nurse, who came out and led Wanda into the room. Wanda stood by the bed and looked closely at the woman's face.

"I can't see her eyes," Wanda said, leaning toward her face. "I can't see what color they are."

The nurse consulted the chart. "She has blue eyes."

Wanda turned and ran from the room, Derek following, then Bruce after a quick thank-you to the nurse. They found Wanda roaming the parking lot, hugging her purse and weeping soundlessly. Derek put his arms around her and rocked her back and forth while Bruce waited for her to compose herself.

"Wanda," Derek whispered, smoothing her hair and kissing her forehead. "We've come a long way. Now we've got to finish it." She nodded and buried her head against his shoulder, letting out a giant shudder before pulling away and looking in his eyes.

"I know, Derek," she said, drying her eyes with her thumbs. She motioned to Bruce. "I think we need to look at that model now."

LATER IN THE MOTEL ROOM, Wanda broke down and cried so hard she thought she might never be able to stop.

Seeing the model, a clay figure that matched Kendall's photograph so eerily in its exactness except for the eye color made her wonder what all this had been about. When she touched it and ran her fingers over its contours, she knew that her daughter's spirit had gone, and she prayed mightily that she might have it back for one more moment, for a second, for a twinkling of an eye.

Kendall was dead now but alive in the hands of the Father, the Son, and the Holy Spirit. It was her only consolation.

The detective had asked that Wanda and Derek submit DNA samples just to make sure, but Wanda didn't need science to confirm what she knew in her heart—her daughter was gone. She had waited too long to hug her and kiss her and tell her the stories she hadn't told her as a child.

As she cried, Derek held her and wept as well, lamenting his own regrets and sorrows. Someone had killed their child, the offspring of a love they knew once and again, a love that gave them strength in the face of their grief.

As Wanda absorbed the shock of truth, Derek had filled in the detective about their daughter's neighbor, and he had taken down the information in detail, assuring them he would do everything humanly possible to bring the killer to justice. Yet that didn't seem as important to her now.

The night wore on, and her tears gradually lessened, as did Derek's, but he stayed the night, sleeping in the chair as she lay on the bed, watching the moon rise through the slightly parted curtain.

"Dear Lord," she whispered, "I prayed for you to guide me, and you brought me here. You brought me to the truth about my child. I know you didn't cause this to happen to her. It was evil that caused this to happen, and I know that doesn't come from you."

She lay there quietly, thinking what to pray next. "Father, I know I prayed before for you to show me what to do if Kendall was dead. That's happened, and I accept it. My mind tells me not to, but I have to because it's the truth and the reality. Now I hope you'll show me what to do next."

So she prayed for guidance through the night until rays of sun replaced the moon, and she rose from her pleas with a new mission, a new calling, and the new heart she had sought for so long.

Twenty-seven

THE AROMA OF HOT WAFFLES FILLED the air as bacon sizzled in the iron skillet. Bruce scuttled around the kitchen trying unsuccessfully to help until Janelle made him sit at the table where he exchanged playful jabs with Daniel.

He had risen early that morning to meet Janelle and Daniel for breakfast. They had been getting together regularly as a family over these last months to smooth the transition for Bruce moving back home.

Home.

All his life he had thought of home as his mother's house, a place where he felt safe and loved, though he hadn't realized it at the time. Now he knew where his real home was, and it frightened him how close he had come to repeating history, to throwing away the two best parts of his life over temptation and selfishness.

"So, Dad, when are we going camping?" Daniel launched into a waffle, and Bruce had to laugh at the syrup dripping off his chin. He looked six instead of sixteen. In a couple of years, Daniel would be going away to college, and the thought that he had missed even a minute of time with this rambunctious, lanky cluster of energy nearly broke Bruce's heart.

"The first weekend your mom and I can get off work."

215

A shadow crossed Daniel's face. "I thought that wasn't going to be a problem anymore."

Bruce sighed. Daniel had made so much progress in some areas. His grades had crept up a notch, and his behavior at school had improved. Some days his anger still flared, though, and he had spent one-on-one time with Rev. Mercer trying to understand what had happened to his family.

Janelle brought a platter of steaming bacon to the table, along with a big bowl of scrambled eggs. "It's not," she replied, shooting Bruce a taunting look.

"Your mom's right. In fact, I've already cleared my weekends for the next month." He smiled at Daniel. The county government had finally voted enough funds to hire a new investigator, and although Bruce couldn't say his workload had measurably decreased—crime never takes a vacation—he felt some of the pressure was off. At least he didn't always have to be on call; someone else was there to take on some of the responsibilities.

As he enjoyed breakfast with his family, he was surprised to realize how much it helped to have a partner, whether it was at work, or at home, or even just in spirit. He had been angry with his own father for so many years that he had forsaken the possibility that he had a Father all along, one that he could go to any time for advice, talk to any time he felt weak or unsure, pray to when he needed solace or guidance. With the help of Rev. Mercer, his mother's advice was coming into focus, and he knew that he needed someone to help him carry his burdens, whether they were at home or at work. He needed to remain vigilant against those things that threatened to take away their happiness.

"So, Dad, you didn't answer my question." He realized his son had eaten his way through an entire stack of waffles and had started on a second.

He looked at Janelle. "How's next weekend?"

"I already asked for the time off," she said, reaching over and grasping his hand.

"Then we're on," he said, feeling happier than he had felt since the first time he saw the girl who became the woman he loved, and held the son who was going to grow into the fine man Bruce hoped he would be.

MARINTHA AND WANDA WATCHED as the nurse showed them how to carefully manipulate Jane's body so she would retain some muscle tone.

Wanda was grateful that Jane had someone to watch over her during the last few months. The pain of not having been there for her own daughter, thinking maybe she could have done something to prevent the tragedy that had taken away her life, was lessening as the days passed.

The day after learning of Kendall's death, Wanda and Derek had made one more trip to the sheriff's department to arrange to bury their daughter. When the DNA analysis was complete, the department would ship her body back to Rawlings where those who loved her could mourn her and celebrate the life she led. She thought it only fitting that Kendall be buried at the place she knew as home.

Afterward, she had asked Derek to make another stop before they returned to Florida.

"Why do you want to go back there?" Derek had asked. "There's nothing you can do for her."

"You know, I realized something out of all this," she replied. "I realized that whatever I can do, I have to do, whether it's for someone I know or someone I don't. Jane belongs to someone, too, and just because I didn't get what I wanted isn't any reason for me to turn my back on someone who needs my help."

"I think it's too soon, Wanda. You might be setting yourself up for more heartache here."

"I'm willing to take that chance."

When they entered the nursing home, an older woman sat in the easy chair reading a Bible aloud to Jane. When she saw them, she stood and came over, grasping Wanda's hands.

"Are you here for Jane?" she asked.

"Yes, but maybe not in quite the way you think," Wanda had said before explaining who they were.

Marintha nodded. "I'm very sorry for your loss. Bruce told me."

"Bruce? You know him?"

"All his life. He's my son," she replied, beaming with pride.

Wanda went over to the woman lying in the bed and placed her hand over the well-manicured fingers. "I can see you've been taking good care of her."

"I can't take the credit. All the nurses and doctors here are the ones who've been taking good care of her."

Wanda looked at Marintha's kind face, thinking how fortunate Investigator Yeats was to have such a loving mother. "I hope I can help take care of her now, too," she said, relating her plan.

"That's such a big responsibility. Are you sure?" Marintha asked, wide-eyed.

"I've never been more sure of anything."

So Wanda had returned home, quit her job, and packed up her things and Kendall's, hoping that if she couldn't use them, perhaps someday Jane could, when she recovered. She had said her good-byes to Lottie and her friends at the Church of the Lord's Disciples and Mel. Sweet, sweet Mel.

"You know if you ever run into trouble, you can still call me," he had said, avoiding her gaze.

"I know," she told him as they left her last AA meeting. At least it was the last one she would attend in Florida. Now she needed to find a group in Virginia. "And I'm sorry about the times I treated you bad. It took me a long time to realize that anyone could actually care about me. You've been a good friend."

Mel smiled. "It took you a long time to learn to care about yourself. That's what made the difference."

Then she made one last stop at Mandy's. Sorrow overwhelmed the young woman, and it was all Wanda could do to bear the grief of her daughter's friend, the friend of her heart and soul.

218

"Now Kendall wouldn't want you to sit and quit," Wanda said, hugging Mandy as tears overcame them. "You have to go on. Kendall would have. She was strong and good, and we have to bring some meaning out of all this. We have to live up to her memory."

"I don't know if I can," Mandy said, holding on to her hand.

"You already do," Wanda said. She took a box from her purse. It contained a gold cross, which she fastened around Mandy's neck. "You were her sister in Christ. Always remember that."

"I will," Mandy said. "I'll never forget her."

So Wanda left, followed by Derek driving a rented moving truck until they reached his small house where they set about remodeling for the new member of their family.

"I didn't think after all these years we'd wind up back where we started, married and starting a family again," Wanda said, exhausted after unpacking all day.

"Do you think we've made a mistake?" Derek looked alarmed.

She laughed and kissed him gently. "We're doing the right thing. The right thing not just for ourselves, but for Kendall's memory."

"Good," he said, wiping sweat from his forehead. "I thought for a minute there I'd brought the wrong woman home with me."

Derek, to the point as usual.

So now Wanda was learning about physical rehabilitation and how to care for Jane. She and Derek had gone to court and won guardianship over this scarred woman, who had begun showing signs of consciousness and an awareness of the presence of others. Soon she would be going home, too. Maybe not the home of her birth, or the home she had made as an adult, but a home where they would love and care for her until her true family could be found.

"I hope that if you find her family, you'll let me know," Marintha said, as orderlies wheeled the woman to an ambulance for the long ride to Virginia.

Wanda turned to Marintha. "Where did you find the strength?"

"The strength for what?"

"The strength to raise your child alone?" Over the last few days, Marintha and Wanda had shared many stories from their pasts. It had been a revelation to Wanda that even a woman who had walked the straight and narrow path felt she had failed her child so badly.

"I spent a lot of time on my knees and plowing through the Word of God," she said, shaking her head. "I didn't always listen for the answers though. I think I ignored them too many times."

"My problem was that I didn't know where to look or who to turn to," Wanda said as they walked behind the gurney. "That's the problem with thinking we know all the answers. We forget there's always someone who knows more."

"I'm glad you're doing this for Jane. If I wasn't getting on in years . . ."

"I know, Marintha." She leaned forward and hugged her new friend. "You have Bruce and Daniel, and I know they'll be fine now."

"Kendall would be proud of you, Wanda. You've turned out to be a good mother."

Jane was now loaded into the ambulance, and Derek was waiting in his car behind it.

"Bruce is still looking for her family," Marintha said, giving her a kiss. "You stay in touch."

"I will," Wanda said, climbing in with Jane. Reaching into her pocket, she pulled out a small brown envelope containing Kendall's pearl pendant. It had belonged to Wanda's mother, then Wanda, before she gave it to Kendall for her thirteenth birthday. Bruce had liberated it from the evidence locker for her.

She leaned over Jane and managed to ease the chain around her neck, settling the pearl in the hollow of her throat. "Rest now, Jane," she said, smoothing her hair. "We've got a long trip ahead of us."

And as the miles stretched on, Wanda watched the woman's face, waiting for that smile she sometimes flashed, as if in the midst of a pleasant dream, and prayed her gratefulness that God does give second chances, just not always in the ways we expect.

EPILOGUE

I wish I could tell you my name.
I wish I could tell you where I lived.
I wish I could tell you how grateful I am
that you came and got me.
Soon I will.

About the Author

Linda Dorrell, a writer and former newspaper reporter living in Effingham, South Carolina, has always loved a good mystery.

When not working on new novels or magazine features (she's written for the national *Southern Living* and *Ancestry* magazines, and the regional *Pee Dee Magazine*), she likes to curl up with novels by Lilian Jackson Braun, Mary Higgins Clark, John Grisham, and others.

Fascinated by stories of true crime, Dorrell has followed tales of missing people and unsolved murders throughout the country. She believes, given the chance, that neither time nor distance, fear nor excuse should get in the way of healing relationships.

She still owns the set of Nancy Drew books that she read growing up.

Visit Linda Dorrell's web site at www.lindadorrell.com.

About the Novel

Although the characters in *Face to Face* are purely fictional and not based on any person, living or dead, the events in a local news report from nearby Darlington County, South Carolina, inspired this book.

The report told of an unidentified woman's body found in a secluded, wooded area. Investigators deemed the woman's death a murder but never found clues to her identity, even after a well-publicized facial reconstruction like the one depicted in *Face to Face*.

No one has ever come forward to identify or claim the deceased woman.

Her murderer remains at large.

During his final week in office, the retiring Darlington County coroner, along with members of the sheriff's department, gave the woman a proper burial in a local cemetery.

ALSO BY Linda Dorrell

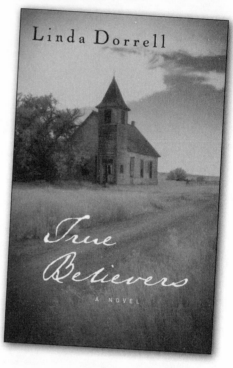

True Believers
A NOVEL

Cotton heiress Peggy
Nickles has bought a dilapi-
dated church and weed-cov-
ered cemetery, much to the
embarrassment of her sis-
ters. As a further disgrace,
she plans to "squander" her
money on fixing it up and
giving it to Otha Lee
Sturgis, a black country
preacher, if he will help
restore it.

Peggy, Otha Lee, and an itinerant carpenter named Joseph begin the
restoration—and are quickly opposed by Peggy's domineering sister and a
racist community. Peggy's sister accuses her of squandering the family
money and threatens to fight for the property deed. The town is out-
raged about giving "white folks'" property to a black congregation. Even
Otha Lee and Joseph become anxious as Peggy seems to break every
social rule of the 1950s South.

While repairing the church and cemetery, the trio uncovers long-held
secrets that put Peggy's true motivation in question. Is she trying to make
up for her family's past or discover it? Are there other reasons for her
determination? Whatever her intent, the small town of Bonham, South
Carolina, will never be the same.